I0534371

Sala The Acolyte

Memoirs from a Parallel Universe

Lawrence BoarerPitchford

Published by Lawrence BoarerPitchford, 2024.

SALA THE ACOLYTE

First edition. October 1, 2024.

Copyright © 2024 Lawrence BoarerPitchford.

ISBN: 979-8988041757

Written by Lawrence BoarerPitchford.

Table of Contents

Chapter 1.. 1

Chapter 2...23

Chapter 3...41

Chapter 4...55

Chapter 5...69

Chapter 6...83

Chapter 7...97

Chapter 8..111

Chapter 9..127

Chapter 10 141

Sala the Acolyte

Memoirs from a Parallel Universe
Universe 9876 X 10^∞
By
Lawrence BoarerPitchford

Chapter 1

The Golans Cometh

"Marjup in a fit of rage over the disrespect men had shown to his daughter Ru, sent his fiery arrows crashing into the world. There was no living soul who was not touched by his wrath. In one day and night, the end of man's hubris came. Those who survived dwelled underground until the copper men came. Those creatures who worship the Metal Mother reared those ragged survivors and taught them how to live again. Among their gifts were the making of bricks, master fire, and how to find and use metal."
~Book 6 of *The Holy Scrolls*, by the priest Ny'ill

A VOLLEY OF ARROWS flew over the wall. Soldiers at the rear of the gate guards cried out, the ice-cold brass arrowheads driving into flesh and bone. A crash vibrated the mighty gate as dust rained down from its stone archway.

Barkov came running up. "The back battlements are nearly out of arrows. I think the Golans are tunneling under the south side wall. If they are successful, they might collapse the stonework there. We are surrounded. There is no way to get past the Golans' main force. It's only a matter of time before we're overrun."

A shout came from the wall near the gatehouse. "Arrows! We need more arrows and sling stones. Bring anything heavy too that we might throw from the battlements!"

Ky called over a soldier from the cohort. "Find more arrows, bricks, stones, or whatever isn't tied down. Get them to the men on that wall!" The soldier grabbed two more men and rushed off.

"I do not like being cornered. There is nowhere to retreat to." Barkov put his hand on the hilt of his brass sword. "We will have to fight, or..." Using his thumb, he made a slicing motion across his throat.

"What? Absolutely not. I am not going to kill myself! When my soul is called to the afterlife, a hundred Golans will have painted the street with their blood at my feet," Ky replied.

The ground shook as the ram hit against the planks of the gate again. On either side, the brass hinges were beginning to warp. The wood cracked. The men just inside the wall jostled back and forth from foot to foot, filled with anxiety and fear.

"That's not what I meant!" Barkov barked. "All I meant was... Oh never mind. How about when the time comes, I cut your throat, and you cut mine."

"If you cut my throat, how am I to cut yours? It is a bad plan. And seems a bit cowardly to me," Ky protested.

A ripping sound came from the gate as a board angled inward. The brass straps cracked one of the metal brackets dangled down.

The few scavenging soldiers returned with buckets of bricks, a few arrows, and some large rocks. They rushed up the ladders and onto the archer's walkway.

"I'm not keen to die, but if it is our time, then this is as good a place as any," Barkov replied as he removed his sword and picked up his round shield.

Ky put sword in hand and kept his shield leaning against his leg. "Where do you get the balls to suggest we kill one another? How many battles have we been in together? How many men have we met in arms and lived to tell about it? You cut your own throat if you are so inclined." He hefted his shield.

"Okay, so no throat cutting. I was merely pointing out the desperate state we are currently in."

One of the nearby soldiers looked over, worry etched into his face.

Barkov smiled at the young man. "Not you, of course. I suspect you'll live a good long life and have many children." He looked up into the smoky sky and saw a host of helen birds, their very presence denoting a grave portent. "Great...the carrion birds gather. How do they always know?" He turned to Ky. "And, no, I'm not going to kill myself. Like you, I'll let the Golans favor me with that task." He looked at the splintering main gate. "Not long now from the looks of things." The board from the gate broke free. "Spears to the gap! Now!" commanded Barkov. "Prepare yourself. They will be upon us shortly."

Six defenders rushed to the breach and thrust their spears through the gap. Enemy screams filled the air as bloody spearpoints drove in and out of the hole. The fighting continued for a few moments.

"Second row, relieve first! First row to the rear!" shouted Ky.

The men at the gate withdrew, and another group rammed spears through the gap.

Ky steadied himself, shield up, and sword pointing toward the enemy. His heart was now quaking, his hands a bit sweaty. "Wait!" he blurted. "A few nights ago, Hydrox the thief told me of a secret way into the city. If it leads in—"

"It will lead out as well," Barkov finished. "He's probably flown already."

Ky looked at the gate as another board was shifting, its metal straps cracked and weak. "Another few blows and the enemy will flood into the city. Murder is in their hearts. I've heard that the Golans do not make distinctions between men and women as they rape."

Barkov frowned. "Who hasn't blurred those lines when conquering?" He looked at Ky with a quizzical expression. "Did Hydrox tell you how to find that secret access way?"

Ky grinned and nodded, causing his helmet to wobble.

"I get the feeling we should follow the thief," Barkov said quietly.

"If we get clear of this fight, to the west is the city of Aul. It has a port and is a big enough city that even the Golans would not dare attack it."

"Aul?" Barkov mused. "There is much wealth there. I'm sure there is a throat cut every day among those narrow streets. I assume they can always use another hand to cut them for brass."

Black pitch sloshed through the gate hole, splashing over city soldiers and the gate boards. Fire erupted and hungrily consumed the wood and men. The battery continued as the smoke and raced up the planks and along the archer's roost.

The militiamen moved back. Arrows flew through the gap and struck several of the waiting soldiers, killing two and wounding two others.

"Don't leave me here for the Golans to torture!" one wounded man pleaded. His fellow soldier pulled him away from the fighting and down an alley into shadow.

"They"—Ky indicated with his hand toward the five rows of militia. "These men are brave, with shields locked, swords and spears glistening in the driving light of the fire disk. But the Golans will crush them. I know it, you know it, and they know it. The only difference is, we are not sons of city fathers, or one of those who have laid roots in this place."

Barkov looked around. "I might have fathered a few here." He frowned and then mused. "They paid us to train these men. It is true they did not pay us to lead them." He looked up into the sky and then down at Ky as the enemy's ram dislodged another board from the gate. "Okay. Your words have bent my ear and lightened my heels. Lead on."

A great rumbling shook the ground as the casing stones around the gate failed. The flaming barrier fell inward, throwing up embers and smoke everywhere. Without delay, the Golans stormed in.

The city militia came together, spears five layers deep riding over every shoulder. Men with shields and swords at the front held the line, thrusting, stabbing, and pressing against the onslaught. Spears did their work, swords tasted blood, and shields splintered, all in the blink of an eye.

"Too late!" Barkov said and began shouting orders. "Watch your right! Spears to the breach! Shield wall press forward!" It was little use.

Both Ky and Barkov moved toward the defenders. A few Golans came around the sides and rushed past the burning gate. Spearmen caught them, rending flesh and blood. Arrows flew through the open gateway. The defenders were falling and being ground under foot by the enemy.

Gaunts, half as tall as a man with six legs and slathering venomous jaws, were loosed by the Golans. The armored creatures rushed in and latched on to a few men, dragging them over the burning gate and out into the fray.

More defenders fell. Men cried for their mothers, their fathers, and their gods. The piles of dying grew in numbers. Several Golans got past the defenders. Barkov cut two down, and Ky intercepted one, leaving him without a leg.

"That line will not hold!" Ky shouted.

There was no denying it. "The time has come to fall back or commit to dying," Barkov called out.

Ky turned on his heels. "This way! And quick is the word!"

"Abandon the gate! Fall back!" Barkov shouted, then followed Ky. "Lead on!" he called to his friend while deflecting an arrow with his shield.

The two friends dashed down the main cobblestone street to the city fountain. An angry mob of Golans' were not far behind, their bloodthirsty screams of savagery filling the air.

"Which way?" Barkov demanded to know.

Ky surveyed the square and interconnecting streets. "This way!" he shouted as the ground shook.

"I hope pillaging will slow their advance!" Barkov said wishfully as he huffed along.

Ky barreled ahead. They ran down a street to a sandstone statue, around a small temple, and down a walking path. A few moments later, Ky started counting side passages.

"One, two, three." Ky turned sharply down the fourth narrow alley. The smell of human waste and rotting garbage drove like daggers up and into his nose.

Cowering citizens stood in doorways protected only by their prayers now. Some, lucky enough to afford a rectangular wooden door, would pile everything they could find up against it and wait for the inevitable. Ky tried to forget that children, women, and the elderly would soon be fodder for the rampaging Golans.

Penetrating deep into the maze of pathways Ky and Barkov zigged and zagged for what seemed like an eternity. Behind them were the sounds of pillaging, the screams of women, the cries of babies, and the clash of implements of war.

Ky turned a corner, following a wide rutted crag partially filled with garbage. He dodged through the twists and turns, heading up an incline, then down into a depression. Abruptly he halted; there was a high stone wall, the city side of the battlements, and a dead end.

"You chiz head!" Barkov chided. "Why didn't you just suggest we throw ourselves from the walls onto the spears of the Golans and spare us all this running?" He wiped gobs of sweat from his face.

Ky mused, "I guess it was the fifth street from the fountain, not the fourth." He turned to Barkov. "Hydrox was very drunk when he told me. 'Fourth' can sound like 'fifth' when one's tongue is numb from much drink. I'll have to remember that next time."

"Next time? Unless the gods take a hand in this, we will soon be knee deep in our own bowels!" Barkov's raised voice betrayed his anger. "We will have to fight in relay. I'll go first. These narrow walls will help keep their ranks useless against our skill. There is a chance that we will send at least forty of them to their deaths before they overwhelm us."

"Or you could live a bit longer," said a voice from behind them.

Ky and Barkov spun around. A man came forth, his dark features highlighted by a sliver of golden light that somehow found a way into the space.

"You've kept me waiting!"

Barkov looked at Ky. "Do you know this soon to be corpse?"

"No," Ky replied.

"This way. Or do you not want to live any longer?" There was a momentary pause. He beckoned them to come.

"You'd better bolt your door and prepare to be welcomed by your god," Barkov warned the mystery man. "The Golans come, and they mean to paint these walls with the blood of those who dwell here."

The man gave a hearty guffaw. "I have no fear of Golans or any other mortal. I've been watching you two. I sent Hydrox to the tavern to tell you of this place. You heard him true, young Ky, for he spoke my words to you exactly. I have a task that calls for two warriors, and I have chosen you two. I suggest you decide quickly, for the Golans even now are picking their way down this street. If you wish to live, come with me. Or you may choose to stay here. A brave man's death is the same as a coward. In the end, both will rot, and carrion birds will pick their bones clean."

Barkov looked at Ky and shrugged.

"Lead on, brother." Ky motioned with his hand, then flashed a sardonic grin.

They both passed through the door. The stranger slammed it shut behind them, then lowered a wooden bar to secure it. Taking a lamp from a wall sconce, he stepped into the dark abode leading the way.

Barkov shivered. "This darkness chills my blood."

"Do you make it a habit of complaining when someone saves your life?" asked the stranger.

"This is the first time such a thing has happened, so I have to say no," Barkov replied.

Narrow hallways and connecting passages came and went.

"You have a lovely hovel," Barkov complimented.

"It is not mine," the man stated. "The person that owns this place is manning the gate...or *was* manning the gate. I see in my mind's eye he now lies in the street, missing a head."

"Who are you? Ky asked.

"My given name is Trecot. My vocation is the Keeper of the Eye. Ah! Here is what you seek...and need." Trecot opened a metal-strapped door and exposed stone steps leading downward.

Ky took a sniff. "Water? How far down?"

"Not far. The old underground river is no more than a hundred paces below us. It still feeds the wells of the city and comes slithering like a serpent under the lands of Shu. Once at the bottom, go upstream. When you've passed the fifty-first well, you will find an ancient access way to the desert. Make sure you fill these waterskins before you leave." He handed the two warriors the containers. "It is the last you will see of water in the coming four transits of the fire disk. Take care as you cross Sol's Oven, or you will become leathery dried husks."

"Leathery dried husks," Ky repeated. "You should have been a poet."

"Are you a sorcerer?" Barkov questioned.

"Some might call me such. Listen...learn...come to enlightenment." Trecot handed Barkov the lamp, and then he grabbed Ky's hand and shoved a piece of metal into it. "Take this. In the valley beyond the Copcu Gate. Far outside the city of Looperland, in the high rocky mountains, you will see an ancient citadel carved into the living stone. Along the cliff just above the river and by the falls, you will come to a door. Use this key to open it. Seek Sala. He is imprisoned there and will soon be destroyed. Free him, and see he gets to Gray Mark. There is a tavern called The Junk. He shall find the path to his destiny there."

"Sounds like a bother," Barkov stated.

Ky looked at Barkov. "A bother? More bothering than being chopped up by the Golans?"

"I'm just stating the obvious," Barkov defended himself.

"There is a reward for you when, or if, you rescue Sala. If you succeed, two chests of brass ingots will be yours, provided Sala is brought alive and well to Gray Mark."

Ky tucked the key into a pouch fastened to his belt. A blast of white light and heat erupted along the hallway. He was blinded for a moment. As the darkness abated, his eyesight returned. There stood a strange man dressed in a dark red robe just a few paces away. Over the figure's shoulder flew a glowing green ball. On a chain that led from the invader's hand to the ground lurched a vicious gaunt snapping its venomous jaws and snorting loudly.

"Ah. There you are. Up to no good I see," stated the stranger.

"Helon," Trecot replied. "Still delivering children to the copper men?"

Helon's eyes drilled into Trecot. "Pray to your new heathen god, Trecot, for I have at last come for you. You have made yourself a nuisance with all your meddling. The Lord of Mech has sent me. The council has watched you from afar as you've corrupted those around you, but no more! I shall teach you that heretics like you will not inherit the world but will only rot within its ground."

Ky and Barkov produced their blades, but their savior motioned for them to stay their hands.

"Your task is elsewhere—not here," Trecot said. "I shall be all that is needed for the rear guard. Now flee!" He pushed them through the door and onto the stairs. The door slammed shut behind them.

The crackling of lightning reached like tree branches from under the door, and a bright blue glow flashed only for a moment. Ky felt the hairs on his bodies standing on end.

Evil and dark words were being spoken beyond the portal, and Barkov and Ky turned and rushed down the stone steps. The shaking of the ground followed them as thunder caused dust to fall from the ceiling.

Their feet slid to and fro on the stairs as hot air rushed past the two warriors.

Ahead, Ky heard the echo of churning water. Before they knew it, both men stood knee deep in the underground river. The cold, crystal clear water rushed past in the dim flickering light of the lamp.

"He said to go upstream!" Barkov reminded Ky.

Ky investigated the lamp's oil reservoir. "There is not much fuel in here. Not a moment to waste," Ky replied and pressed forward.

The water was loud in the confines of the tunnel. Several times, they waded up to their chests. Barkov held the lamp, whose flame caressed the arched roof, leaving long streaks of black soot.

Along one of the bends was a hollowed-out area with a sandy alcove. Both men stood there for a time to regain their strength.

Ky took the small terracotta lid off the basin of the lamp and looked inside it. "The oil is growing low. We'd better find those wells soon."

Barkov's eyes betrayed his concern. "Agreed. I'd hate to be trapped down here with no way to see." He climbed back into the water and began pushing forward against the current. Ky followed.

A short while later, Ky saw the first shaft of light. As they approached the eerie glow, a jug tied with a rope plunged into the water right in front of them, and just as quickly, it was retrieved up the shaft and into the daylight above.

For a long time, they sloshed their way up the canal. Ky counted out the circles of light above as they came and went. Just as he counted the fifty-first one, they found a raised bank and a tunnel leading upward.

The flame of the lamp was growing smaller when they came up on a wall of stone with a ledge twelve hands high. Barkov helped Ky get on top, handed him the lamp, and jumped up and grabbed the ledge. Just as the lamp ran out of oil, they saw a simmering light piercing the darkness through a crag.

The rough, jagged entrance led to a set of worn carved stairs going down to a stone-strewn wadi. The riverbed had steep banks and was deep in the middle. Barkov and Ky slid down into it.

"Which way now?" Barkov asked.

Ky looked along the dry waterway. "It slants downward. So that way."

The two men began walking.

The fire disk arched toward the horizon four times as they walked, camped, foraged, and sparingly consumed their precious water.

Following branch after branch of the winding river canyons, the two warriors did their best to avoid the fire disk's savage heat. The smooth walls of tan, brown, red, and black striations made the pathway mesmerizing.

"The sorcerer's warning to be wary of the water remains fresh in my mind." Barkov looked up at the steep walls.

"Sorcerer? Did he say he was a sorcerer?" Ky asked.

"Only a man manipulating nature could have such knowledge as he espoused. Only a wizard would have caused the ground to shake as we fled. Oh, he was one of those creatures the copper men so covet alright," Barkov said.

Ky looked up into a wedge of light and shielded his eyes. "No birds, I see. Never a good sign." He lifted his waterskin and drank a bit. "Don't worry, old friend. If you exhaust your water, I have enough urine to sate your abundant thirst," Ky offered without a hint of humor.

Barkov took a swing at Ky, but the smaller, younger man nimbly dodged the blow.

Ky ran a few dozen paces ahead along a patch of light. "Not so fast, friend. You'll be consuming more water if you persist in trying to brain me!"

Barkov grunted his disapproval. "Perhaps I'll open one of your veins and drink your irreverent blood after you've fallen to slumber." He sat against a wall and slid down.

Ky sat back. "Most likely, you will only find dried powder in there now."

Both men laughed and then became quiet and serious.

As the fire disk hit midday, the shade in the canyon was barely a sliver. They sat there for a while, and then Barkov stood and took the lead. He followed a meandering bifurcation that seemed to angle downward. After a few hours, it led to a small box crag, where piles of debris formed a dam. They climbed over the mass and were surprised to see in the distance the mud-brick walls of a small city straddling a dark green river in a vast plain.

"Is that Nor Frangu?" Ky asked.

Barkov narrowed his eyes and stared for a moment. "Seven towers along the wall... I think it's Vara Goon, City of King Narcies. Yes, it is Vara Goon alright. I can see the white dome of the Temple of Con."

Ky shaded his eyes with his hand. "I see it. Not too far now. Unfortunately, once we strike out, we will be directly under the fire disk."

"The fire disk has no pity for fools, so expect none. Come on. If we make good time we can be there by early evening."

KY AND BARKOV WALKED on as the fire disk dipped behind the desert mountains. The moon gods, Herod the Red and Marjup the Green, took the disk's places in the sky. Around Marjup was his great bow, arrows loaded in the quiver just off his shoulder.

Herod, on the other hand, glowered with his massive oblong eye, which was only visible from time to time as the spinning red of his brow came and went.

"There they are," Ky said.

"Who?"

"Marjup and Herod. I wonder if it is true that Marjup sent fiery arrows crashing into the world."

"Don't be so gullible," Barkov scolded. "We are men, and we are still here. So were our fathers, and their fathers."

"Still a good story," Ky stated.

Barkov stopped, drew his blade, and crouched. "A pack of remas stalk something near that dark patch of land ahead." He pointed using his sword.

Ky followed Barkov's weapon. "I count six."

Both men knew the dangers of remas. The beasts hunted in packs. They scoured the deserts, near places of water, for their prey.

"They're heading away from us now." Barkov licked his finger and held it up. "The wind is against us...the little wind it is. Let us give them plenty of room to find better victims than we." He moved at an angle away from the creatures and then headed toward the city, paralleling the river from a safe distance. "If we travel fleet of foot, we can be at the gates before Marjup is beyond the horizon."

Both men took off at a jog.

The moons vanished, and shadows began to stretch from the far mountains as the fire disk rose above the lofty peaks to the east.

Not far away were the tall gates of Vara Goon. Ky and Barkov followed a worn path that cut through the sand down to the hard limestone. Others wandered the path too. Men with pack animals, women with children, slaves, traders, whores, entertainers, and scholars all traveled the road in hopes of trading goods and services behind those mighty walls.

An old man suddenly spoke to Ky. "Do not be one of the unlucky who commit crimes. The inquisitor here is cunning with his tortures, and if you survive, a slave you will become."

The old woman by his side spoke too. "It is important to avoid violating the king's laws, even if it means suffering the insults of a belligerent drunk, the berating of a haggler, or the reprimand of a priest or cleric. Do not let your wild ways betray you."

Barkov did not reply. Ky nodded and smiled.

Ky learned at a young age to follow the rules inside walled towns and cities, even if on occasion he flagrantly disobeyed them for his own ends. It was Barkov who had more trouble in places of noble control. His nature was to teach those who disrespected him a brutal lesson so they would not make that mistake again. The man called it a civic service.

"You!" shouted a soldier at the gate. "Come forward!"

Ky approached.

"What do you bring for the good of our city?" the guard asked.

"I bring wisdom, my labor, and some ingots of brass," Ky told the armed man.

The soldier looked at Ky's weapons, though they were not out of place. "Wisdom?"

"Yes. I've traveled far and for a long while, and now I crave rest and entertainment. I plan to trade news for coin or use my skills for board and a patch of straw."

The soldier grunted as a pedestrian somewhere down the line waiting for admittance shouted for the line to move. "Very well. Come in. Learn the city rules, or you will regret not obeying them." He shoved Ky toward the tall wooden gate and looked at Barkov. "You! Come forward!"

Barkov approached. His large but lithe body dwarfed the guard. "What?" he asked.

The guard looked Barkov up and down and stepped back. "Be good. Don't fight or cause damage. The rules apply to you as anyone else who wanders the streets. You can go in."

Barkov stepped past the soldier and entered the city.

"Why the grin?" Ky asked.

"I enjoy the initial fear a man feels when I stand over him brimming with naked power."

"Just the size of you warrants a man's caution. At least he did not learn of your more deadly skills," Ky said.

"Or more lustful habits." Barkov chuckled. "Come with me. I think I remember a tavern not far from this gate. If memory serves me, it was stocked with courtesans, mighty jars filled with beer and wine, and...many yards of star root."

Ky perked up. "Star root? Are you sure? Or is it that you were far too drunk to even remember what soft, pale, brass bearing lout took you as a courtesan?"

Barkov shoved Ky ahead. "You have not the constitution to know what pleasures a soft, pale, brass bearing lout might provide a man such as I. The truth is as shocking as it is a fantasy. So, onward soldier, until drool leaks from your lips as you stew in the sweet, dusky cloud of star root and wine."

Ky chuckled as he picked up his pace.

Ky and Barkov stalked the streets of Vara Goon. Ky asked an old man where the closest wine bar was. The old man, his hand shaking, pointed down the street across the market square, toward a mud-brick street leading to a lath-and-mud structure topped with a thatch roof. "Visit the Garl Och."

"Good!" Barkov pronounced.

"What is good? Garl Och means severed hand," Ky stated.

"The tavern is next to a large temple. I am sure that some of the finest flesh peddlers will serve both institutions."

"So, they make a pretty pair." Ky replied. "Watch someone doesn't steal your hand while you sleep...or copulate."

As the fire disk came directly overhead, they crossed the loud and bustling market. Colored awnings of red and yellow were flopping in the breeze as plentiful as sails in a harbor.

Barkov lay his hand on one of the wooden columns that was holding up a red awning. Painted in black along the wall next to the door were the words 'Garl Och'. He lifted the latch and pushed the door inward.

Inside, rough-hewn tables and stools were strewn around, and the space was full of entertainers. Jugglers hurled flaming sticks back and forth. A magician conjured tiny people and set them on a table. Gawkers watched as the small images danced to mystical music that came from several minstrels atop a narrow raised stage. A mighty and ruthless-looking fellow with one eye rolled some dice and then grew furious as the tiny amount of brass in the betting circle was claimed by another. In a flash, a knife came out, but was met by a heavy pot of stone, and the looser crumpled to the dirt floor and was hastily removed through a back door. Nude women and men strutted between the tables, offered their bodies for pleasure and brass.

Intermixed were rough-looking blokes and dangerous-looking female warriors. Most wore some form of metal blade, and none looked as if they should be abraded with disdainful language or their patience tried.

Barkov charged directly through the throng, found an upended table along the far wall, and righted it. He brought over a couple of stools and planted himself on one. Ky sat opposite him.

"Bring six jars of wine and two reeds of star root. We will have a couple of women as well. And, while you're at it, bring roasted meat and bread and beer!" Barkov demanded of a man rushing about with an earthen pitcher filling drinking bowls with beer.

The man seemed to take no notice of the warrior until Barkov reached out and stayed him by his arm. Looking Barkov over, the weary fellow gave him his full attention.

"Yes... Meat, wine and—"

"Star root!" Barkov ordered.

"Of course. Two reeds of star root. Immediately." The proprietor rushed off through a door in the back, shouting for some help and praying no harm would come to him.

In a flash, several young men—no doubt the sons of the owner—came rushing in with a dish heaped with greasy meat, two loaves of bread, and an armful of small wine jars.

Using his knife, Barkov chopped a hunk of meat away from the bone and slopped it into his mouth. Next, he tore the lid from the wine and consumed a healthy amount in a single draft.

Ky was more subtle. He cut some meat away, folded the bread around it, and took a mighty bite. Once he swallowed, he lifted the wine jar to his lips and drank heartily. He then reached into his leather pouch, pulled out an ingot of brass the length of his thumb, and put it on the table.

One of the sons looked at the brass with surprise before snatching it up and rushing off to his father. The elder came to the table.

"This is far more than I can take for your food and drink," the proprietor exclaimed.

Barkov lowered the jug from his mouth and wiped his lips with the back of his hand. "Keep it. We will be here for some time. You will earn that brass. I saw you have a stable in the back. We will be residing there for a few days."

The old man thought for a moment. "Very well. You are welcome here. But this is not an inn—only a tavern." He paused, looking at the ingot. "Yet it is true that owing to your generosity, I welcome you as I would my own family."

It was clear that the old man was genuinely surprised by the amount of brass and was invoking the code of local hospitality.

Ky nodded. "You bless us with your generosity." He bowed slightly.

The old man flashed a mostly toothless grin. "Good. Good. It will be an honor to have such men among my family." He turned and went back out the door as his children brought more food and drink for the warriors. Then came the star root.

Chapter 2

Wandering Star

"The baby Kyachi is docile—easy to fool into trusting you. An adult Kyachi will trust no man and will kill one if able. A wise man will never try to fool a Kyachi; for mother or child, to think you smarter than they is to die a thousand deaths." ~Book 19 of *The Holy Scrolls*, words of Biblio Dy the Wise

BARKOV AND KY SPENT the next few days indulging in the pleasures of the city. They drank much, took a woman each, ate heartily, and smoked the pungent star root until their eyes glazed and their minds swam within golden rivers of the gods.

On the fourth day, they sat at a table in the Severed Hand, discussing whether they should press on and find the man named Sala or divert toward the west to a brewing battle against the Golans. Ky lifted a jar of wine to his lips as two big men dressed in common garb strolled in and toppled a few tables.

"Where are you, Pilat?" a man with a dark scar down his face shouted.

Ky put his wine down and looked on.

The old proprietor came rushing in from the back and immediately prostrated himself to the men.

"Forgive me... Business is bad. I was going to send my son to Shae Kah today. Pray forgive my lateness!" Pilat groveled.

The man with the scar pulled his pants down and proceeded to urinate on the old man and then on the upturned tables, narrowly missing Barkov, and Ky.

The other man, who had thick black hair and a beard, took out a knife. He gripped Pilat by his urine-soaked hair and put the knife against his nose. "I'll just take the end off to remind you to pay on time."

Black Hair let go of Pilat, let out a rattling from his breath, then jerked wildly, dropping his knife. Behind him stood Barkov, and three inches of the brute's sword protruded from the man's chest.

Scar turned, surprise in his eyes. His head fell onto the wet floor and rolled against one of the tables.

"Unruly," Ky said while wiping his blade on Scar's shirt. He smiled at Barkov. "Well accomplished. You got him through both the lungs and heart."

Barkov swiftly withdrew his sword and let Black Hair fall to the ground. "Get up, old man," he said to Pilat. "No one disrespects our family."

Pilat rose to his knees, his face a mixture of terror and shock. "What have you done?"

Ky placed his sword in its scabbard. "You have made us part of your family. It is only right that we make you part of us. As Barkov said, none shall treat our family with such disdain."

"But these men are messengers of Shea Kah. Shea Kah will have my eyes, and the eyes of my children!" Pilat cried.

Barkov turned to Ky. "Well, if Shea Kah is the problem, then we go to deal with Shea Kah. Be calm, Pilat. Ky and I will sort this for you. It is not well known, but Ky is a master at rhetoric and negotiation. Rarely does our encounters turn to bloodshed." Barkov picked up the dead man's head, and he and Ky left the tavern.

Pilat paced the floor in terror. He bemoaned and cursed the gods for sending the warriors to his drink house. Then, he cursed the gods for his bad business investments. Then, he recanted all.

"Please, Marjup, god of war, of the hunt, and of cunning, spare my children and my wife. Let Shea Kah kill only me."

The great fire disk began its dip toward the far hills. Pilat managed to remove the bodies before the afternoon crowd came for their evening wine, beer, and food.

Just as he was scurrying around filling bowls with recently brewed beer, he saw the two warriors darken his doorway again.

"Why torment me, you gods?!" Pilat cried out.

"What is this, old man?" Barkov asked as he entered the tavern and tossed a head onto one of the tables. "Here. Ask forgiveness of Shea Kah in person. I am quite sure he will listen to you, for we kept his ears where they have always been."

Ky entered, his clothes and face covered in congealed blood. "It appears that Shea Kah has no longer a need for your paying tribute. He and most of his henchmen are seeking counsel with the gods now. My list of problems solved by use of rhetoric is unblemished."

Pilat looked over at the head and gasped. He looked away then back. "He...he is dead?"

"As dead as the parlak you cooked for us this morn," Ky replied. "You have no need to fear him now. Consider it a gift from your adopted children. We killed his lieutenants as well."

Barkov laughed loudly. "Your children. They can rest easy now."

Ky looked around at the startled patrons. "I see you removed the bodies. Good, for they will bloat quickly in this desert heat."

Barkov went to sit down, but Ky stayed him with a hand on his arm.

"Two men who sat near the door have rushed off," Ky stated.

"They run to call for the city guard," Pilat said.

"Barkov and I have overstayed your hospitality. If you prepare us some meat and cheese, we will take our leave," Ky replied.

The old man rushed out of the room and returned with wineskins and food wrapped in a cloth bag. "Here, before the city fathers come for your heads," Pilat told Ky and Barkov.

Barkov strolled over to the doorway and looked out. Down the street was a group of ten men in lacquer-braided armor carrying shield and sword. Their gaze left no doubt that they were heading to Pilat's.

"To the east along the wall, you will find a place where the water flows into the city through a tunnel. At the end is a heavy wooden grate. It is loose, and you can force it open and escape into the desert beyond," Pilat told the two warriors. He grabbed Ky by the arm. "It is probably of little use to tell you, but I suspect you don't understand what rhetoric is."

Ky shrugged and took the sack. "Maybe not, but your issue is resolved." He and Barkov fled out the back and down the street along the wall. Behind them, they heard raised voices.

It took them only a few minutes to reach the river inlet. They ducked into the tunnel through the wall and came to a set of copper rods forming a grate.

"No wood, but metal. Do you think old Pilat set us up?" Barkov asked.

Ky pointed to a circular wooden grate propped up against the side of the tunnel. "There's the old one. And it's made of wood. They must have replaced it recently."

Voices echoed. "They fled this way! I am sure of it!"

"Okay, if ever the gods loved either of us, let it be this day." Ky threw himself at the rods, placed his feet on the lower ones, and pulled with all his strength.

Barkov also grabbed the metal bars, and after only a moment, they bent. He pulled the two middle vertical bars, and they, too, slowly gave way.

"Can you fit?" Ky asked Barkov.

"Yes!" Barkov slipped through the grate, followed by Ky.

"Wait!" Ky called. "We must force them back into shape."

"Bend them back?" Barkov looked on the verge of outrage, but then he saw the logic in it. "Very well."

They forced the bars back into place, though they looked a bit warped and the mortar holding them in the wall fractured and rained down.

From down the tunnel came a shout. "Light a torch and follow me!"

Barkov leapt to the side of the water access and moved down the wall a few feet. Ky did the same on the other side. The flare of the flickering yellow light cast shadows of the bars on the water.

"They couldn't have come this way. The metal rods bar the exit," said a deep masculine voice.

"Come! They must have gone down an alley. Find them!"

The flickering light vanished; only darkness remained. Ky and Barkov remained still and quiet for some time. Eventually, they crept along the bank of the estuary and out into the desert.

By the time the fire disk began its climb into the sky, Barkov and Ky had logged many miles. As the heat began to grow unbearable, they found a cave and ducked in. Along the land, the wavering and brutal heat flew from the sands back into the sky, causing the surroundings to look distorted.

The two men drank wine and ate some of the provisions.

"How far to the Copcu Gate?" Ky asked.

"So, it is decided. We will seek this Sala for that wizard," Barkov stated as he wiped wine from his chin.

"It seems the thing to do," Ky responded. "Do you know of this place called Gray Mark?"

Barkov thought for a moment. "It is a walled city to the west. It lies along the northeasterly trade routes and was built in the mountains where the bubbling springs of the Slog feed the headwaters of the Cu'thul River."

Ky sat back. "That river flows into the Blackheart Sea. Boats sail it as far as the lakes of Gruber. Have you ever been to that city?"

"Once, when I was younger. I was sold to a man who made warriors to sell to warlords and chiefs in the south. That is how I learned this trade we wield," Barkov told Ky. He lifted the skin to his lips and drank again.

"You never said that before."

"Never came up," Barkov retorted. "Nonetheless, I think we have four- or five-days' travel to reach the mountain gates. There, the land will change, and you will see a forest and rushing rivers of white froth. In the high peaks, white flakes can fall from the sky, and it is bitterly cold. It is vastly different than the desert."

Ky thought on this in silence. "When the fire disk dips, we shall away." He put his head on a rock and covered his eyes with the crook of his arm. "Probably best that we rest. Many days still to travel."

When night came, Barkov and Ky traveled far and fast under the glowering light of the two moon gods. When dawn finally found the travelers, they were dashing from oasis to oasis along the Nubar trade route.

They encountered the Marduk and Hushtus tribes, whose long animal trains, stocked with spices, food, and rare wares, flexed, and slithered like tahut worms in search of victims to devour. Several times, the two gruff men sheltered in the hillside cracks of fractured stone as a band of Marduk drove their large brown shaggy hanaks and scaly drooks along the narrow gorge and toward a shaded mesa watering hole.

The great beasts lumbered along the stony path, their thick, hairy hides protecting them from the oven-like heat of the fire disk. The Marduk traders scanned the hills and shadows for bandits, never once spotting Barkov or Ky.

As the topography changed from sand dunes and desert hills to gray granite slabs and rolling grasslands, Ky and Barkov broke from the trade route and turned directly west.

Far upon the horizon, they saw the large snow-covered peaks of the Beroakridge Mountains. There, in those lofty, white-capped peaks, several gates of shattered granite and limestone pointed toward Gray Mark.

Six times the fire disk came and went. On the seventh rise of the fiery orb, Barkov found a cave, and they made camp in the mouth. They rested through the heat of the day. As the two moons began their rise into the clear and star-rich sky, the warriors made a small fire and ate.

In the shallow rocky valley, Barkov found several rubert plants. He dug up the roots and returned to the cave. After cooking, the two companions feasted upon the dark purple roots. Barkov knew the sweet and savory flavor would satisfy them all night and into the next day's travel.

Ky ventured out and discovered a clump of squat, shaggy cockle trees. He stripped the peeling red bark and made his way back to camp. He took out a small copper cup, added some wine, and then mixed in some crumpled bark. Tucking it into the coals of the fire, he let it heat to a boil. As it cooled, he took a drink and then passed it to Barkov, who did the same, then passed it back. The flavor was rich and spicy. Both men felt the powerful energy from the tea driving their heart and filling their limbs - compelling them to break camp and take to the trail.

As dawn broke, the desert dunes began to fade into the distance. The men pushed up into the tree-covered foothills, avoiding the small hamlets that were scattered about the bubbling brooks and small rivers that came down the slopes.

Along their path were occasional hunters; these bandy men and women supplemented their meals with barcat meat and the flesh from the plump and plentiful furry horned yonks who grazed on the leather bush and the tall, coarse grasses dotting the hills.

Barkov blazed a trail through the forest, across the flower-studded meadows, and up into the craggy rocks of the mountain. By the third day, the chill in the air was growing bitter, and Ky untied the pocket inside his shirt that contained his cloak.

Donning the garment, he watched Barkov chuckle at him. "You think you're freezing now. Wait until we are atop the true mountains!" A biting wind came up, and Barkov's eyes narrowed. He reached under his shirt and into a hidden pocket there, removed a cloak, and tied it about his shoulders.

Ky raised an eyebrow.

"It is because I did not want you to look foolish wearing that thing if we were to come upon a wandering shepherd, peasant, or tradesman," Barkov explained.

Ky only smiled. "If the great Barkov leads us into the company of anyone by mistake, then it is not the great Barkov who stands before me."

Grunting his discontent, Barkov again moved up the hillside with speed. Ky stayed in his shadow all the way up.

When the sky became filled with light, they looked upon the first gate along their journey. Not much more than a crag gave way into the mountain stone. The V-shaped pass was less than a dozen paces wide.

"Once beyond this pass, there will be two more, then we will reach the Copcu Gate," Barkov said.

"Keep your wits about you," Barkov suggested. "Though the giant was slain many long years hence, his kin still stalk the land up here, I have heard. Warn me of anything you see that is strange. If it is a giant, we must run to find a shelter to hide in."

"That is unlike you," Ky began. "I have never heard you speak like that. What sort of creature can strike such fear in you?"

"This area is so named for the mountain giant Trampic eui Copcu, the vicious creature that devoured mountains and shat out precious metals for the ancient kings. When the time is right, I will show you his remains from a distance. Then you will know and tremble with fear at the thought of a beast such as that roaming the land devouring mortals like we," Barkov warned.

The two men ventured between the pillars of the gate, which was made of rough and shattered stone, sixty feet high, and almost four broad paces wide. They moved past it slowly and silently and then followed along a path that had been trod by few over the years.

Once they were on the other side, the smell of smoke caressed the crisp air ever so faintly. The path led to a ledge that was above the trees and overlooked a small valley populated with a deep and dark forest of ancil trees.

"Somewhere within that dark wood roams drifters, bandits, and those who wish to remain hidden, until they are upon travelers," Barkov warned. He knelt and brushed away some dirt, exposing a tightly placed square of paving stones. "The old kings and queens once thought highly of this pathway. But now? It is said that those who dwell in this forest are not welcoming to strangers. If you hear or see anything, give quiet warning and we will melt into the trees."

The road had many switchbacks, climbing for a while towards the lofty peak and then descending. By nightfall, the men had gone through the dark woods and up the second mountain, arriving at the second gate.

Beyond was the valley known as The Limeral. In the middle stretched a long beast of a river.

"Those waters are white with froth," Barkov said. "It will betray a man's steps if his foot is not planted well. There." He pointed along the winding serpent of water. "That is the walled city of Gimble. If we travel hard through the day, we can be in a tavern beyond those walls before dark. There, we can take respite and satisfy some of our more driving urges," Barkov suggested.

"I can surely do with a meal of fresh bread and meat. I would not shirk a drink made of local berries or beer of local grain either. Maybe even a woman to warm my bedroll," Ky mused aloud.

"All of that and more await us," Barkov replied as he broke out into a jog down into the wide valley.

A host of small farms littered the expanse. Hearty billet seeds were being grown on some of the land, and rows of various nut and fruit trees were being cultivated on others. The main road passed through the middle of the farmlands and straight up to the main gate of Gimble.

From afar, Ky saw farmers, hunters, entertainers, slave traders, and more, all converging on the mountain city. Ky and Barkov slipped in with the masses.

The guard at the gate simply waved them in. The poor fellow definitely had his hands full with the caravans and produce-carts from the surrounding farms waiting to be taxed.

Once inside, the two men made for the market, an octagon-shaped open space. From there, they followed a staggering tradesman to a tavern.

The sign on the door showed a jar of beer and a leg of meat, and Ky was ready for both. A small green awning hung over the door. Barkov lifted the latch, pushed the door in, and strode into the dark. A somewhat sour smell assaulted his nostrils as the interior of the bar came into focus.

"We have some of the freshest beer in the city," claimed a fat man with a blue-beaked tuturk on his shoulder. "Show me your ingots." He looked Ky up and down as if he were a piece of meat. "Or will you be offering trade of a different type?"

Ky slapped two small bronze bars on the table. Each was divided along its axis by four deep grooves, and the pieces were no longer than a large man's thumb. "We pay with metal," he said. "Bring four jars of beer and a hind of hurak meat!"

The man looked at the brass with an almost lustful gaze. "Perhaps rich men such as you might be interested in our berry froth wine, made with the finest spring water, crushed local semus berries, and left to be blessed by the woodland spirit of drink and passion. What say you?"

"Bring it!" ordered Barkov.

The proprietor snapped into action and gave a shout, and before Ky could sit, the drinks were on the table.

"The meat will be coming. We must bake it in the traditional grease pan so the skin will become crispy. Oh, the gristle will make your mouth lust and your bowls freshen!" The man turned nimbly on his heels and vanished into the crowd.

Ky and Barkov spoke for some time. The meal was brought, and they feasted. By the time they finished their last jar of berry froth, the light outside was long gone and the taverns lamps freshened three times with oil. Ky looked about; the place was nearly empty.

The large barkeep stood near a tub of dishes, providing physical punishment with a cane for any broken dishes as two young boys worked furiously to clean them all.

"You! Fat man! Where is there a stable or inn to be had?" Barkov demanded.

"Out the door, to the right, down the street. You will see a large stone hand in the middle of the road with its finger pointing up to the gods and the thumb out to the side. Look to where the thumb directs you. There, you will see a door the color of the sky. It is called The Giger's Rest. The owner is a friend of mine. If you say I sent you, he will find you a room and give you protection through the night for a meager price." The large man never turned around.

They exited and began following the barkeep's directions. Soon, they stood at the base of a carved marble hand twice the height of Barkov. To Ky, it looked as if it had pushed its way up from the darkness of the underworld.

Barkov looked up. "Where do you suppose it is pointing?"

Ky followed the thumb to the side. "Who cares? Look, there is a blue door. Must be The Giger's Rest."

To the right of the sea-blue portal was a golden cord. Ky pulled it, and somewhere within the building, a bell rang. A moment later, a tall man with an eye patch unbolted the door and pulled it open.

"Who are you?" the tall man asked.

"I am Barkov, and this is Ky. We seek a place to lay our heads for the night. Stable or bed, we can make do with either."

"The fat man at the tavern sent us," Ky added.

The innkeeper thought for a moment. "Do you pay with trade or metal?"

"Metal," Ky said. "The tavern keeper said something about a favorable accommodation."

"Ah! Liden sent you! I see. You will have a room." The innkeeper put out his hand and waited.

Ky fished out the smallest bit of brass he carried and placed it in the man's hand.

"Okay, welcome to my inn. You will share a room, and do not cause trouble. My wife makes a morning meal just before dawn. You are welcome to join us." The innkeeper stepped aside and allowed them to enter. Once they were inside, he closed the door and used two crossbeams to secure it. "Follow," was all he said.

They followed him down a narrow hallway to a room at the end. Inside was a stone floor, a grass-filled mattress, and a table.

"Good sleep to you, and may you rise with the fire disk," the innkeeper said.

LIGHT FELL UPON THE dull yellow wall of the small room. Barkov woke Ky and they made for the inn's kitchen. They made short work of the breakfast, then bid the innkeeper fare tidings. Next, they found an outfitter.

"We will take the woolly boots, leather trousers. Give us two carry sacks, and enough food and drink to get us past the mountains - provided we foraged and hunt a little," Ky told the proprietor.

Having stuffed their packs full, the two warriors left the city and headed along the valley road toward the far snow-covered mountains. As the fire disk dove into the abyss of night, Barkov and Ky reached the foot path leading up to the pass just below the glaciers.

The stars twinkled above in the inky blackness. "Look," said Barkov. A cabin waits for us."

A lit lantern at the door flickered an orange-yellow light about the wooden portico. Voices and laughter bubbled from within.

A snort drew Ky's attention. Up along the trees was a large lean-to. Inside, a crowdok stood hunkered down tied to a post. The beast, which was as tall as Barkov at the shoulder, had its wings folded, and its armored feathers glistened in the light of the two moons. Just beyond in a pen, several luknars, free of their luggage, feasted upon highland grass and white-topped cleet flowers.

Barkov stepped under the moss-covered porch and threw open the door. A dozen men and women in animal skins, shawls, and capes, stopped and looked, then went back to drinking from horn cups and cavorting. A roaring fire consumed logs in a stone pit, its clay chimney allowing the smoke to escape through the side wall and into the night.

A man with a long, dark-black beard approached and shoved a cup into Barkov's hand.

"Welcome to Lower House! Drink. Take part in the joy, for if you travel over the pass, tomorrow you may run into dead as you climb!" The man gave Ky a drink, slapped him on the back, and laughed hard. When he calmed down, he grasped Barkov by the arm and said loudly, "I am Gu Mal, the keeper of Lower House. You are welcome for as long as you need." He looked at their packs. "Seems you are prepared to climb the mountain. I hope one of your bags contains an icon of your god. He will no doubt be needed if you see Trampic and his brethren!"

Ky drank down the contents of his cup. Gu Mal pointed him to a set of tall wine jars against one of the walls.

"Drink your fill, traveler!"

On a table was a storage jar tipped on its side. A wooden pipe stuck out from the top, and a cork kept the liquid from rushing out.

Another patron stood and, upon tenuous legs, made his way to the wine station, where he removed the cork, put his cup under the spigot, and dispensed some dark blue liquid into his cup. He then replaced the cork and staggered back to his seat by the fire.

"Wine is good. I do have a powerful thirst that needs slacking," Barkov stated, and headed over to fill his cup again.

Ky followed. Once refilled, he lifted the cup to his lips. It was sweet—as sweet as the thick mucus made by the flying chree bugs in the low valley hives. After a few drinks, Ky began to feel separated from his body. He moved about the cabin and found a long table by the fireplace.

He set his cup down, turned around on the bench, and eyed the blaze. The glow was soft, with colors dancing and hovering about the flames. Dark blue, penetrating orange, and iridescent red coals dominated the flames.

The crackle was loud, but there was something else there. A cadence...a voice, distant chanting trying to tell him something desperately important. The words were unintelligible—perhaps an ancient language he did not understand. From the licking flames, music followed the voices.

He looked across the room. Barkov was throwing dice. The man was nearly twice as tall as anyone there. His dark hair was short and shimmered in the light of the lamps and fire.

Darkness consumed Ky's vision, then he was looking at himself sitting at the table. There were others suspended there too, hovering in the room. He looked up to the roof and watched himself fetch more wine, drink it, sit again, and put his head down on the table. The chanting voices were getting louder. The image was fading. Ky was fading. In a moment, he fell into a pit of blackness.

Chapter 3

Birds of a Feather

"In the depth of our most desperate hour, the Inc came forth and, with unflinching decisiveness, chose three of the children. They were taken to the Great Hall and presented to Sheal, the sorcerer maker. In, one by one, the small babes went, sealed in by a stone lid so their screams could not be heard. In and out came the metal arms, and they were forever altered to walk the world, possessing the power of the ancients."
~EXCERPT FROM THE WRITINGS of Ye'et the Dark Monk of Fuor

BARKOV WOKE TO THE chirping of birds. He sat up. The harsh smell of firepit smoke, sweat, and sex filled his nostrils. He clambered up and sat on the raised hearth of the fireplace. His head was fuzzy, and he needed some water.

As he got to his feet, he noticed Ky lying slumped over the table. In fact, most of the people from the night before were in a similar state.

He stumbled outside, and the bite of the mountain air nipped at his skin as he made his way to the water barrel, drove his fist through the ice, and scooped some of the crystal-clear liquid into his mouth. Instantly, his stamina returned, and he stood tall.

He looked along the trail and up at the snowcapped mountains. He consumed some more water, found the latrine, relieved himself, and then went back to the cabin. Gu Mal was outside at a cookfire, where the flames furiously consumed the chopped wood.

"In a short while, there will be much food to feast upon. You'll need a stout breakfast to sustain you for your travel up the mountain," Gu Mal said. "You'd better wake your fellow traveler. Both of you will need to make an early trek if you are to avoid the looming storms."

Barkov looked into the azure morning sky. "I see no clouds or portents of a storm."

"I feel it. And I'm never wrong," Gu Mal stated as he put his culinary ingredients into a large copper pan and stirred.

Ky appeared at the door. He gingerly stepped forth and staggered to the water barrel. After sating his thirst, he came to where Barkov stood. "A harrowing night to be sure," he said.

Barkov contemplated this and nodded, followed by a grunt.

"Dreams haunt you?" asked Gu Mal.

"Dreams I have had. A monk came to see me, then I saw the place where they dispose of them. Horrible. More horrible than a Yimagus' torture chamber," Ky said.

"You must have the blood born from those who once came from the crucible," Gu Mal told them. "The mountain berries can have that effect on those whose mothers came from ancient stock."

Barkov grinned. "There is something new I discover about you almost every day. Usually after you've drunkenly made a fool of yourself, and strangers tell of it to me."

Ky scoffed. "I am not of such a pedigree. I come from the southern clans and the town of Jur. We are hunters, warriors, gatherers of the forests, and keepers of the sacred places."

"The wine does not lie, my friend. But I am sure the gods will reveal to you the truth of your life when the time is right," Gu Mal told Ky.

Ky folded his arms over his chest and made a dubious expression while looking at Barkov.

All the visitors ate inside the cabin. The sky grew dark with clouds, and by the time they finished, a mist danced in the forest treetops. A dozen men and women began to put on their cold-weather clothes, boots, and gloves for the challenge ahead.

Gu Mal waited on the trail. He rode a black shaggy luknar. Half the travelers had animals, which had packs loaded on their backs or saddles with riders mounted. The travelers who didn't have animals walked through the knee-deep snow.

Ky and Barkov fell in line with those who did not have personal transport, and their journey up the mountain began. After an hour, the snow began to fall, though the air remained still.

"Curse this cold!" complained a man a few dozen paces ahead of Ky. "It bites my flesh and stings my cheeks!"

A woman looked back over her shoulder at the complainer. "You'll stay warmer if you keep that hot wind inside instead of spewing it out for the gods to hear." She turned her gaze ahead again.

Barkov looked back at Ky with a twisted grin. "She speaks to my heart. I wonder if she has a lover."

Ky chuckled. "Perhaps she could ride you like a luknar, swatting your ass with a crop to keep you focused on the path of her desires."

"It is like you can see into my wish and make it flesh!" Barkov laughed, puffing out clumps of steam from his lungs with each guffaw.

For hours they slogged through the growing white drifts. Then, as darkness began to settle, Gu Mal struck up a torch. Down the line of travelers, torches were lit. The ground glowed yellow with the flames, as it blanketed the hillside trees in shimmering shadows.

The wind picked up and bent the flames back down the trail. The moon gods seemed to be hiding above the clouds, plotting mischief against the mortals below. In the distance, an orange glow appeared—a lantern hanging at the door of a cabin.

"Smoke. Seasoned logs burn just ahead," Ky said to Barkov. "There!" He made out the rectangular structure. The animals with riders were bunching up, their torches showing the moss-covered cabin roof.

Gu Mal reached the door as the frigid wind began to blow hard. He pushed the door in and was greeted by a boisterous voice.

"Welcome to Halfway House!"

Ky was surprised that the voice belonged to a lean and muscular woman. She wore her hair long, and it was the color of the brilliant purple hygros flower, whose petals glowed softly in the dark of night.

"I am Freya. Come. Put your animals in the cave up along that trail." She pointed along a dirt leading into the woods. "Then, come in and sit by the fire. The storms are moving in, and soon the snow will reach the eves. The wait shan't be long, and soon you will reach Top House and be on your way into the next valley."

Ky saw the long knife at her side; it was a deadly tool that no frontier folk would be without. She was shirtless from the waist up and wore only a scant fur skirt about her middle. On each foot were rawhide fur boots laced up to her knee.

The cabin was warm, and with all the people inside and the white hills growing outside, all the travelers began to shed their heavy clothes, until not a soul wore a stitch.

As night approached, Freya propped the door open with a log to cool the room. She opened several tall amphorae of wine and two barrels of beer and then took a horn cup. "Drink...and rest," she told them.

Ky noted that as the evening wore on, Freya used less fuel for the blazing fireplace. As the weary travelers ate, they spoke of adventures and deadly encounters, and they even told a few ghost stories as the winds battered the log structure throughout the featureless night. Before the snow blocked the door, Freya removed the log, closed the structure up, and then lay down on a fur rug by the still-red coals of the fire.

Barkov and Ky laid their bedrolls along the wall not far from the hearth and reclined, resting upon one arm, as they listened to the others.

A beefy merchant spoke. His eyes scanned those bathed in the ghostly yellow glow of the fire.

"My grandfather—may his old bones feed the fire disk—told me of the roving copper men. How they came from afar and crept into the tents of the new mothers. Upon floating feet, they lurked, and from the sleeping babes, they chose the healthiest of the newborns.

"As luck would have it, a slave was attending the night watch and screamed in terror. For his valor, the copper men paid him with a bleeding throat and made straight for the camp's edge. My great-grandfather took up an axe, charged one of the fleeing horrors, and struck the copper man hard. But it was useless, for the monster stopped not and, in a moment, vanished into the black night to climb the burning stair and deliver their ill-gotten goods to the mother god of metal."

The room was silent for a moment. Many knew of the copper men. Few had ever actually seen one. Ky thought about this for some time. He'd heard the stories from his own clan. In his youth, they'd scared him—made him obey his parents and elders—for it was common knowledge that the copper men came to take those children unworthy of their families and will them away into servitude for a hideous monster called the mother god.

A young woman fetched a panyar from her carry sack and began to pluck the vertical strings. After a few twangs, she burst forth in song. She sang for a while, the melody soothing and passionate.

Ky's mind drifted. Slowly, the coals of the fire melted into visions of battle as his imagination became fertile.

The woman stopped playing after a time. Freya shoveled the last of the coals into a few warming jars and set them around the room. She then climbed into her bed and lay down. "Sleep well. Fear not the copper men or wild beasts tonight." She wrapped herself in the animal skin and went to sleep.

Ky listened in the darkness. The muffled howls of the wind outside and the battering of the walls reminded him that nature was powerful. He closed his eyes and fell into a deep slumber.

KINDLING AND WOOD SNAPPED and crackled as the flames grew in the fireplace. Their hostess was up doing chores as Ky and Barkov rolled up their beds and secured them by their packs. Others were awake too, and all made ready to leave.

The fire disk's warmth came upon the cabin. Freya opened the door, waded out into the snow, and returned with a bucket filled with ice. She set down the bucket by the fire, where it melted into drinking water. She then placed some frozen meat on skewers and set them over the licking flames.

"You will all want to get going as soon as the meat is cooked. Take it with you as you travel. Do not delay, for the weather up here is without pity and can change in a moment," she stated.

Ky and Barkov took up their packs and the food then made for the door. Looking back into the cabin, Ky thought of Freya. She was lovely, but clearly not one to be reckless with. So, he had chosen not to approach her for carnal pleasure. Yet, he now regretted not taking that risk.

More travelers came out, some preparing their riding and pack animals for the journey. From the cave that served as a stable, the beasts were loaded with their owners' goods and led out onto the trail.

Barkov blazed ahead, tramping down the snow along the switchback trail up the mountain. Few wild animals were about, and only once did they see a wandering bull arck pulling ripe lipy fruit from the high bows of the jaka tree. The large shaggy male took little notice of them as they tromped past.

It took most of the day to reach Top House. The structure was larger than the last two, with a three-story stone tower on one side. Here, a detachment of guards milled about along with a tall broad-chested blond-haired man wearing furs.

"Travelers! Come hither and warm your hands and feet. I'm Yu the Bold, and I will prepare you for the descent into the valley past the Copcu Gate." He waved them onward up the snowy path to the front door of the long stone-and-wood structure. "For those of you with animals, follow the path marked with wooden poles to the cavern stables. There, your pack creatures will be kept warm, watered, and fed for the night."

The main part of Top House was wide with a firepit in the middle. Logs were piled high as the flames leapt toward the roof hole, from where the smoke raced out.

Barkov noticed the floor was smooth stone without joints. He was mystified by this, for he had never seen the like. "How is it there are no flagstones underfoot?"

Yu addressed Barkov. "We built this place upon the very stone of the mountain. It is that which you trod upon. There are no tiles or slate...or dirt, for that matter." He laughed a hearty guffaw.

As the other travelers filtered in, Yu assigned places around the long structure for them to set their belongings and bedrolls. When all were inside and the door shut, he directed all to long rough wooden tables and benches. There, they were treated to a feast of steamed roots, various breads, baked mushrooms, and copious amounts of mountain berry red wine. When all was consumed and more wood piled into the pit, the jars of beer were brought out and their tops removed. Each traveler was welcomed to dip a cup into one of the jars and drink their fill.

As before, those who felt inclined began to tell stories of far-off places and great battles. Outside, the howling wind added to the ambiance as the door rattled with every gust.

Once the stories had run their course, those who were tired from the travel and heavy with libation found their way to their sleeping places, where they curled up for the remainder of the night. Barkov and Ky did the same, and before long, the darkness of sleep swallowed each, biding its mysterious time until the fire disk would rise and release all those from its otherworldly reality.

BARKOV WOKE. HIS HEART raced as the visions of a giant lumbering toward him faded away. He struggled to his feet and retrieved some of the stale beer from a half-empty jar. He made his way to the door and stepped out into the glorious morning sunrise. The bright red-and-orange light bathed the land with the coming of the fire disk. No clouds remained above—only an ever-growing blue hue beating back the darkness. He walked over to the edge of a stone cliff, pulled down his rawhide trousers, and did his business.

Below stretched a landscape of clouds to the horizon. He was sandwiched between those brooding white balls of fluff and the great kingdom of the sky god.

"Beautiful, is it not?" Yu asked, coming alongside him.

"Such sights never fail to render me one with the gods," Barkov replied.

A breeze came up and the mist below parted. A dark forest stretched out to the distant mountain peaks.

"Most mornings, I look upon this sight. In the spring, one can see the valley below and the dark greens and bright yellows of the forest. There." He pointed down at a dark oblong blob. "That is Rangar Meadow. The yellow and red flowers stretch like meandering rivers to the distant mountains. It is a blessing to behold. There is not a day that passes that I don't rejoice in this view," Yu stated.

Barkov put his member back into his fur pants and looked over at Yu. "You are a man in his prime. Why is it you do not take up sword and shield and fight in the wars that surround these mighty mountains?"

Yu chuckled. "I am much older than you know. I have done my time fighting the wars of men for gods and kings." He looked off into the distance. "That holds nothing for me now. I have earned a life of peace and service to my fellow travelers of the world. Here, I and the others maintain the trails and lodgings. When we can, we pass along our wisdom to those who pass by. We are provisioned by the surrounding cities and live out our lives in good stead."

Barkov thought on this. "Perhaps in a time beyond my thinking, I might feel the same. But today is not that day, as my sword thirsts for Golan blood and my heart lives for the quest." He gazed into the distance one last time then turned and went back inside.

Ky packed up, slung his pack and sword, and stowed his waterskins. Barkov did the same.

When Yu came in, he prepared the morning meal and doled out extra provisions for the last leg of the journey into the lower realm.

"Stay together until you reach the walled city of Looperland. Once there, go your separate ways, and may the will of the gods guide you further," Yu told them.

After they ate, the column of pilgrims and traders started out, heading downward. Slithering from the trees came a mist. The ground became very wet, and moisture clung to every surface.

As the heat of the fire disk came upon the land, the mist burned away. The smell of moss and wet soil filled the air. With each step, the snow brightly reflected the god's light.

They traveled all day and into the coming evening. The cloud layer came and went, casting cold shadows upon the land. Darkness settled, and a freeze came upon the travelers. Ice was forming on each person and animal as they approached the tall wooden gates of Looperland.

Passage through the city gates seemed only a formality to Ky as each traveler was waved through by armed guards. Once inside, Barkov and Ky broke away from the caravan and headed for the first wine house they could find.

A lithe, dark-haired woman greeted them. "Welcome, lads. Find a table and tell me what will slack the thirst of travelers from afar."

Ky found a rough-hewn table and sat on a stool. "Bring me a cup of wine," he told the woman.

"I'll have a beaker of beer," Barkov ordered. "And bring us bread, cheese, and any meat you are cooking for the day."

Once the woman was away, Ky turned to Barkov. "Since you've been in this area before, do you have any idea where this ancient citadel is?"

Barkov thought for a moment. "No. I've ventured toward the east a few times as far as the remains of the giant. There are no roads that go that way. The temple must be beyond the place where the giant lays."

"Have you seen the giant – really?" Ky pressed.

"Few have traveled there, and when I was here last, I had to see the beast for myself. There are only animal trails through the thick brush and woods that lead to the giant."

The woman came by and handed them their drinks. A moment later came a platter with the food. Ky placed an ingot of brass on the table, and the woman's eyes widened.

"What hear you of an ancient structure carved into a mountain?" Ky asked.

"Stories... I hear to the east, where the mountains form a place called the Cupped Hands, it is said that there remains the giant who stands guarding the temple of Marjup," she said. "But it is not a place pilgrims go, nor is it a place where our people venture."

Ky took a drink. "Why not go there? If it is legend, do you not want to see it for yourself?"

"None travel that way, for there is no pass over the mountain—no roads or trails leading there. Those few who did once seek the old ruins, they never came back. The old ones say the copper men dwell there. It is a place where sorcerers are taken to be made into dust. I have no interest in such things. I leave it to legend for legend's sake."

Barkov broke off a piece of brass and slid the small token to the lady. She quickly snatched it up and put it into a leather pouch at her side.

"We will call you for more drink soon." Barkov waved her away.

Ky took another drink. "How many days' travels to get to this giant you speak of?"

Barkov thought for a moment. "Three days, I think."

"We should get provisions for two weeks and a couple extra waterskins. Also, let us get two bows and a good supply of arrows. We will need them, I'm sure," Ky stated.

"In the morning," Barkov said. "Tonight, we shall sample the evening festivities of Looperland."

Chapter 4

Liberators

"#684: To disable the controls on the DNH Protocol module, select the 'Administrative' link. Once done, choose 'Settings,' and find the 'Admin Release Protocol Controls (ARPC)' switch. Once done, activate the ARPC. You will be asked to provide authentication credentials. Plug in the wetware connection and wait for the authentication approval ocular visor indicator. Once verified, place the DNH selector switch into the 'Disable' mode. WARNING: Any attempt to override the authorization credential step will prove fatal."
~SCRAP OF HOLY SCRIPT, dated before the Arrows of Marjup.

IT ALL STARTED WITH beer and wine. Then came the star root. Later, there was some brawling and then a harrowing escape from the town guards. It was all a blur for Barkov and Ky. When the fire disk rose, the two warriors crawled forth from behind some crates and grain sacks in the town market and made their way back to the tavern. The barmaid brought two jars of stale beer and beakers of thin wine. Both men drank and ordered an abundant breakfast, after which they prepared to depart Looperland.

The guard at the gate gave Barkov a hard look as he passed. "You! Were you out last night causing trouble?" demanded the armored man.

Barkov shook his head. "Trouble?"

"Yes. Two men as large as you and your companion. Where were you last night?" the guard asked.

Shrugging, Barkov looked off into the distance. "My fellow traveler and myself merely arrived in town last evening and had a good night's sleep to prepare for our journey today. You can see we are carrying enough for a long travel."

"Many days we must be gone," Ky added. "We certainly had no time to cause trouble last night."

The guard's face betrayed his doubt about Barkov's story. "Very well. Be off with you. But if I find out you two were fighting in the brothels last night, we'll extract a confession with hot irons!" He waved the two warriors through.

Cold winds blew about the woods as Barkov and Ky headed east. Drizzle came and went as they exited the trees and entered a wide, grassy meadow. The musky scent of loam and peat was strong, and more than once, they had to circumvent large dark pools made from bubbling springs that fed nearby brooks.

The thick, mulchy soil they slogged through often came up to their shins, and every now and then, a bloodworm would surface, flop about in the muck, and then descend again into the depths.

After some time, the ground rose a bit, and they found that their boots were growing dryer. The incline increased as they walked. Trees grew in thick clumps, gobbling up the space for the grass and dominating the land.

For two days, the warriors went up and down rolling tree-covered foothills and around stilted locks filled with light-blue waters. The traveling was hard, and each night, they made an open fire and roasted what food they had foraged along their path.

Great shadows grew as the fire disk rose into the sky. Barkov stopped and surveyed the land from the shore of one of the lakes.

"There...toward that rise of stony cliffs in the distance. There, we will see the giant." Barkov then began moving around the lake toward the cliffs.

By the coming night, they had made it to the top of one of the jagged hills. There, they camped again, repeating their pattern of preparing for supper, posting a guard, and sleeping in shifts.

By morning, Barkov woke to a blood red sky. "Come," he said to Ky. "You will see and always remember this sight." He led Ky to the ragged edge of the cliff and waited as the shadow slowly gave way to light.

Ky watched intently as a beam of white from the fire disk landed upon the shoulders of a mighty monster. It was slumped, facing the V of a mountainside. Trees and brush clung to the top of its head, upon its shoulders, and along one arm that grasped the dirt and stones across from its gaze.

"I never imagined such a sight. The gods... How could such a thing live? What did it eat?" Ky whispered.

Barkov chuckled. "It appears to be dead or asleep. We'd dare not wake it, for if it were to stand whole and complete, it could reach us up here with little effort."

"It is burned into my memory as truly as my own name." Ky watched for a few minutes while Barkov went back to the firepit and buried it with wet dirt.

"Come. Let us find this temple the wizard spoke of." Barkov stated. "Let us see if we cannot put this Sala onto the path his guardian so desires." He shouldered his pack and waited for Ky.

Once both were ready, Barkov led the way along a narrow animal trail that zigzagged up along a mountainside stream. The churning waters lurched and bubbled, falling into descending pools.

The ice and patches of snow came and went. Further up, Ky saw caves in abundance. They made their way towards one of them.

As night came on, they lit a torch and entered the gaping hole, stalactites hanging down, stalagmites pushing upward – both men likened it to being swallowed by some monstrosity. Inside were the expected sights—rubble, animal dung, a long disused fire ring, and some charcoal sketches upon the walls.

"Look here." Ky shone the torch about the old images. "Looks like a drook, and over here is a Kyachi." He held up his hand to one of the red handprints. "About the same size..."

"Let's collect some wood to burn. It will be cold tonight," Barkov said.

Ky moved a bit farther into the cave. "It's warm to the touch along this wall."

"Warm?" Barkov approached. "By the gods, it is. How strange. I pray it is not a sorcerer's cave we have wandered into."

The fire blazed at the mouth of the cave. Barkov took first watch. He sat near the front with his sword over his lap. His eyes scanned the mountain ledge as he listened for the sounds of approaching feet.

He grew tired and stood. The fire was burnt down to coals. Looking outside, he saw that the two gods were high in the sky. He turned and went back inside. Nudging Ky with the toe of his boot, he spoke. "Wake. Your time to watch."

Ky rubbed the sleep from his eyes. "Right," he said.

Moving to the firepit, he sat there with his sword on his lap and tossed in a few sticks. Barkov went and lay upon his bedroll, and promptly began snoring.

Barkov relieved Ky a couple of hours before dawn, allowing the man to get a little more sleep. He took the time to prepare some food from their provisions. At dawn, they trudged on.

At midday, Ky signaled for them to stop. He pointed up along the mountain. It was as plain as daylight—a temple carved into the gray rock.

"Well," Barkov said surprised, "Herod be praised that we came upon it." He looked about. "How do we get up there?"

"Come on." Ky made his way up and toward the enormous structure.

They followed the stream for some time until it stopped at a broad, deep pool, where water plunged from the high cliff.

"It will not be easy. The rocks look jagged and loose up higher," Ky stated.

"There." Barkov pointed. "Steps carved into the stone."

"Clever indeed," Ky added.

After climbing over large rocks and wading through ice-cold water, they came to a substantial beach of rounded stones. Just a couple of long strides away was the start of the stairway. Slowly, the two warriors began to ascend.

It was not easy, for each tread was wet and narrow. Carefully they rose, until both men were on a ledge overlooking the pool a hundred feet below.

"Another set of stairs," Ky said pointing.

This access was more like a ladder, as the angle was very steep. Though the stone lips were dry, they required one to pull up with one's arms and push up with one's feet.

Barkov crawled upward, drawing himself up with his powerful muscles. Ky followed, and the two soon stood at two tall bronze doors securely locked. Some distance away from the mighty columns that marked the front of the temple was a path.

"Somewhere along here is a door?" Ky mused.

"Perhaps," Barkov said under his breath. "This way."

They followed a trail leading away from the front, until they came to a fissure in the mountainside. There, the two men found a door strapped with brass, and a heavy metal loop dangled at the side.

Barkov tried pulling on the loop but could not budge the portal. He then tried kicking it but found it immovable.

"Now what?" Ky asked.

Barkov thought. "Didn't that wizard give you a key?"

Ky chuckled. "Indeed, he did. I completely forgot." He pulled the odd bit of metal from the pouch at his side. "I don't see a hole for the key."

"Try the handle. Maybe there is a hidden slot there," Barkov suggested.

Ky held the loop up. A small black square was there. The key glowed brightly, then there was an audible click. He pulled the door open. Darkness met their eyes.

"The lamp," Barkov said.

Ky poured a bit of oil into the lamp's reservoir then lit the wick.

The glow illuminated the entrance and the narrow walls on either side.

"What do you smell?" Barkov whispered.

"The stench of pitch, lamp oil, burnt metal, and people," replied Ky.

"This place is inhabited. Let us hope there are few to no copper men," Barkov whispered.

Once they crossed the threshold, Ky closed the door behind them. Into the blackness they trekked until Ky stopped. "Listen."

Somewhere down the tunnel, a constant humming echoed. Barkov touched the wall. "It is vibrating." He put his ear against it. "I hear voices too...chanting. The words are foreign to me."

"Keep moving. I don't want to be caught in this narrow passageway," Ky said.

They proceeded. The tunnel was as straight as a spear shaft. The voices became louder, and soon, the two warriors were at another door.

The smell of burning oil and dust was rife. Ky took the key, reached under Barkov's arm, and pressed it against the square below the ring. A click echoed.

Barkov gently pulled the door inward, and a flood of light cut into the darkness of the tunnel. Beyond the door, a pungent smell, like that of a hot spring or pitch well, overpowered all other odors. He peeked out.

"It is a wider hallway. Wait!" Barkov closed the door.

Footsteps came, and the marching of those in lockstep was accompanied by the clacking of metal. It took a moment for the sound to fade. Again, Barkov pulled the portal open.

The two men slipped into the other hallway and evaluated the path: odd smooth walls, a strange floor, and glowing areas along the tops of the walls as well as the floor.

"Magic," Ky said under his breath.

"A side tunnel, follow me," Barkov commanded.

They turned down the branching hall, which ended at a shaft with a ladder leading downward. As the sound of shuffling feet approached, Ky blew out the lamp.

The two men watched from the dim light of the glowing wall. A procession of robbed figures marched past. Each had a circlet of glowing metal around their head.

One of the figures stumbled and fell. They all stopped.

"Damn you, Corgor! To your feet. The pool you will not avoid by falling down!" A large figure wearing a cowl stood with his back to Barkov and Ky.

Another prisoner, gold threaded tassels dangling from his robe, reached down and helped the one called Corgor up.

"A blessing be upon you, Sala," said the prone figure. "I do not wish to die!"

The large, hooded fellow stepped forward and, with the force of a brute, held Corgor and forced some liquid into his mouth.

Corgor coughed, putting up no true fight. He swayed and then stared ahead as if dazed.

"To the chamber with you all," the hooded man said.

The group shuffled off. The large figure followed.

Ky and Barkov looked at one another, their hands resting upon the hilts of the swords at their sides.

They quickly moved to the passageway and watched the figures turn right into another hallway. The two warriors followed at a respectable distance, never allowing the figures to fall completely out of sight.

The group went down a ramp to a door and filed through it. The portal closed, and Barkov and Ky stood at the entrance.

Barkov put his ear to the impediment. "They're moving further away. Use the key."

"Who darkens our door to the sacrificial room?" a deep voice asked behind them.

Ky spun around, as did Barkov. A large, robbed figure with burning-red eyes glowered at them.

"You lack the markings of the chosen. You are from the outside and have stained this place with your filth!" The figure reached for them with metallic claws.

Swords flew from the two warrior's sides. The blades bit into the advancing enemy, but they struck something solid with a loud clack.

"You will be reduced!" said the attacker. "Your essence will be used to make anew those failing circuits." The figure latched on to Ky and lifted him from his feet. Ky struck repeatedly with his sword but to no avail.

Barkov threw himself at the attacker and, with all his might, wrestled with the unnatural thing.

Ky dropped his weapon and gripped the cold metallic hand. The crushing grip began to render him lifeless. In his panic, he lashed out, tearing the cowl off. A hideous sight came to view.

Even in the midst of the fight, both warriors gasped loudly. Ky fought harder.

"Copper man!" Barkov shouted in shock. A fit of raw panic came over him as the hair on the back of his neck stood on end. He tore the arm from the horror and wrenched it from Ky's throat. In a moment, he beat the abomination savagely with both his sword and the dismembered arm.

The copper man fell back. The creature's burning eyes turned to Barkov, and it came for him. But just as it latched on to the fighter, Ky flew onto its back and, with brute strength seen only in men facing certain death, tore it from its metallic shoulders.

The copper man spun around, sparks shooting from the torn, flailing colored sinew. It fled down the hallway but collapsed just before reaching the end. Ky turned to pursue it.

Barkov grabbed his arm. "It is vanquished."

Ky turned to the door. "If we are to rescue Sala, we must with fleet of foot do it now." He spun around, and in one motion, he took the key and pressed it against the door.

Barkov pulled it open, and they descended into a dank, stinking tunnel.

A few moments later, they came out onto a high ledge overlooking a cavern wrought from the very guts of the mountain. In the middle of the chamber was a giant box made from walls of glass strapped with green tarnished metal at the corners.

Both men kept their swords out. Robbed figures were lined up. Two were on a set of metal stairs leading to the top of the glass enclosure, and a copper man stood at the top, lowering one person at a time.

Inside the box, the person stood on a metal trestle. They stepped down onto a stair, then dove into what appeared to be a clear liquid.

To Barkov and Ky's horror, the person and all their clothes dissolved into nothing. A horrible stench was in the air; it was like that of a tannery or dyer. The next sacrifice was lowered in, dove into the substance, and was gone.

"There. That's the one they called Sala."

Ky looked at Barkov. "Surprise and savage force are our only hope. Let us drive hard upon the enemy as we did at the battle of Rolling Hill."

Barkov nodded.

The two men crept down the ramp from the ledge. The assembled were facing away from them. A copper man was acting as gatekeeper, allowing only one at a time to advance up the stair to their death.

Barkov gave Ky the nod, and they rushed into the enemy with enough force to knock ten over upon the charge.

Ky waded through, grabbed the man with the gold tassels, and drew him back toward the ramp. The metal monstrosities engaged Barkov as he fought a retreating battle back to Ky.

Up the ramp they slashed, kicked, and bashed. Black fluid coated the ground as Barkov slew the enemies. One fell and then another. He focused on their head and neck, for it was the only place that appeared to be vulnerable.

One of the monsters came forth with fire-red eyes, and from under his clothes, he brought out a tube made of metal. Barkov and Ky felt their life force draining as the creature brought the tube to bear upon them.

Both men fell to their knees. The copper man reached with his empty metal hand and pulled back his cowl. The glowing eyes pulsed with light and the skull-like face shifted its brass-colored jaw back and forth like a saw.

Barkov clutched his head and growled in agony. Ky was down on his elbows, the slick black fluid coating his limbs as it dripped down the ramp toward the abomination attacking them.

"Your meat will be stripped from the bones," the coppern man said without moving its mouth. "Submit!" It stepped up the ramp toward the now prone Ky. Then, it wobbled, the legs flailing as the feet slipped wildly.

The tube moved to the side, and Barkov, without hesitation jumped forward driving his boot into the monster's chest. It slid back rapidly into the crowd and smashed into another copper man.

Ky got to his feet, grabbed Sala, and pulled the young man up the ramp to the door.

He flung open the portal and ran straight into four copper men, knocking them to the ground.

Ky dragged Sala over the top of the metal creatures as claw-like hands grabbed for them, but he did not stop. They trampled the prone creatures and dashed down the passage. Barkov was right behind them.

"This way!" Ky shouted, and all three found the side passage. They came to the door, the hallway, and the exit. The key opened it, and the three of them stumbled out onto the path leading to the waterfall. Ky slammed the portal shut and then drove his dagger between the frame and the door, securing it in place.

"That should hold them for a time!" he said loudly, then rushed after the fleeing Ky.

Chapter 5

Lost Wits in the Wastes

"Born of fire in the darkness, the Kime and Chote came forth. The copper men of the age continued their labors for those smote by the gods. Kime and Chote dredged the world of all the relics that would guide the powerful to rule this land. A maelstrom of battles came. The copper men did battle with those who lingered from in the ancient cities. The wizards, witches, and nobles chose the path anew and, in so doing, allied with the men made of metal and lightning to defeat the old and breathe life into a new age. Then, when the globe was poised to be at peace, the wizards marshaled against one another and drove man back into the holes in the deserts, mountains, and forests, where he would scratch out a life like animals, eating carrion, licking his wounds, and dying in great numbers as the ice and cold crushed the world."
~EXCERPT FROM THE *Book of Hides*

HALFWAY DOWN THE STONE stairs, Sala stumbled and fell against Barkov. Ky attempted to grab Sala, and in doing so, caused all three to tumble over the slick rocks. Planting at the bottom in a crumpled heap Barkov leapt up, pulled Ky and Sala to their feet, and drove them like herd animals along the river.

"Move, you fools!" Barkov chided.

After dashing over the smooth round stones of the estuary, all three men came to another falls.

Barkov skidded to a halt. The stony edge dropped away more than a hundred hands. Green and churning white water rolled over the ledge and fell through a mist into an obscured pool below.

Ky spotted a narrow animal trail and led the way. "Follow!" he commanded and plunged down the path.

Once on the ground, they followed the roaring river until the fire disk began to fall away, driving the land into darkness.

Barkov halted. "I've gone about as far as I care to," he declared. He looked back at the way they'd come, then loosed his sword. "If they fall upon us, we will have to battle them as we are."

Ky surveyed the area. "Into the cover of the river foliage," he called and promptly hid. "Better for an ambush."

Barkov followed, pulling Sala along as if he were a sack of produce.

Nothing came along the riverbank. Nothing came searching through the woods nearby either. They all stayed silent and motionless for some time. As the night creatures began to sing and call out, Ky spoke quietly. "Let us find a meadow or clearing in the woods. Someplace to shield a fire and defend if necessary."

"Defend?" Barkov scoffed. "We shall fight like a Kyachi protecting its young—with purpose and surprise." He put his ear to the ground. "Though I hear no one following on our heels."

"How can you hear over the racing waters?" Ky asked.

"I can hear!" Barkov retorted.

"They...they come not for us," Sala said. "They think me not worthy of a pursuit, it seems. They know that none will give me shelter or supplies for miles for fear of the copper men."

Barkov and Ky stared at the young man. He had not spoken since they'd rescued him. Both had forgotten that he was even with them.

"You speak?" Ky questioned.

"I am just now gaining my mind back. The control circlet has fallen off my head, and the *vgrut* they gave me that clouded my mind is waning." Sala sat down on a large stone. "Who are you, and why would you risk your lives to bring me from the Chamber of Recycle?"

"Recycle?" Ky asked. "What word is that? What does it mean?"

Sala went to the river's edge, cupped his hands, and drank. When he was done, he spoke. "Recycle means to reuse. Within the Chamber of All Things, a being can be recycled into our base components. Metals and elements can be extracted and used for other things."

"Very odd," Barkov said. "You are filled with metals and"—he thought for a moment— "elements? Like fire, air, water, and land?"

"Yes. All things are filled with such, including you," Sala said.

Both Ky and Barkov broke out into laughter.

When they stopped, Barkov said, "No wonder I feel so heavy all the time."

Sala sighed. "The amounts are so small you would not be aware of them."

"I wonder how much brass is in my great pile of dung?" Barkov furthered. "Next we are in a city, I shall see if I can trade some for drink and use some to gamble with!" He laughed hard.

"I would pay an ingot to see that!" Ky replied and broke out into a hearty guffaw.

"That is not how it works," Sala told them. "So, why did you rescue me?"

"A stranger saved our lives and bade us to find and secure you," Ky replied. He spun around and stared into the thick trees. "I smell helliomot fungus, and they always grow in circles in open clearings."

Barkov smiled. "If you smell fungus, then lead us to it."

Ky led the way into the darkness of the woods along a nearly imperceptible path, the type only a skilled and experienced tracker could decipher. As Ky predicted, an opening of nearly a hundred paces across emerged from the canopy. Grouped in the middle were dozens of circles of tan mushrooms with red speckles.

Barkov gathered some wood, and they made a camp inside the farthest edge of the forest. The two warriors dug a pit, put a stone over it to shield the light, and then made a fire.

Around the hidden blaze, they built a circle of pointed branches, then made nests for each to lie on for the night.

The two fighters shared their provisions with Sala, and they drank from the waterskins before the fire had burned down to just coals.

Barkov stood. "I'll take the first watch. Get some sleep if you can. Dream of lusty women with ample bosoms and cauldrons of sweet honey wine." He vanished into the darkness around the camp.

"Why does he leave us?" Sala asked Barkov.

"If those who hunt us find our camp, where best is it that a guard be placed?"

Sala thought about this. "In the darkness around the camp, not within."

"Of course. Thus, Ky is now in the wind and wilds, and there he will stay until it is my turn to play sentry."

"Clever," Sala said. "I have much to learn from you folk of the green wood."

Barkov nodded, then lay down with his sword unsheathed and in hand. "Try and sleep. We have hard travel ahead come tomorrow."

The cold was settling in, and Sala shivered. Ky came out of the darkness and directed him to take a large stone from the coals, place it next to his nest, and cover it with some dirt and loam. For many hours, the hot stone kept Sala sleeping well.

Barkov relieved Ky and throughout the night, came in and out of the camp putting small twigs and bark on the fire before vanishing again into the brush and trees. The wind kicked up, and for a time, it felt as if it would rain, but the sky did not weep, and the scathing bluster weakened to nothing.

Sala heard Ky get up and Barkov lie down. He drifted in and out of sleep. The drugs were nearly out of his system, and he was finding it hard to have any dreams. After a time, an image began to form, a mighty beast chipping away at a hillside with a tremendous pick. Sala was flying into the thing, and he became aware that it was not living, but a machine. There was a place near an array of colored lights. He took his hand and laid his hand-tattoos along a black-glass window.

"Come on. Let's get a move on." Barkov's voice was calm but commanding.

Sala opened his eyes. His stomach groaned, but he did not complain. He struggled to his feet, stretched, and then noticed that the camp had vanished. Nothing remained, save for his nest.

Ky looked at Sala. "It is not good to be in the habit of leaving traces of one's camp for an enemy to track."

"How?" Sala asked.

"Consider this a lesson in how to learn to live and survive as long as you can in the greenwood," Ky said.

"What now?" Sala asked.

"We make for Looperland," Barkov said.

"What is in Looperland?" Sala asked.

"It's the city we recently came from. We will need to get you outfitted if you are to survive the long trip to Gray Mark," Ky added.

"Take this path." Sala pointed at an animal trail. "It will lead us to the giant."

"Giant?" Barkov said his eyes narrowing.

"Fear does not become you, oh fearless warrior," Sala stated and took the lead.

Ky shrugged. "I don't like this."

Barkov pushed Ky forward. "Just follow the lad."

THE THREE MOVED DOWN the steep mountainside and came to a rushing river nearly ten paces in width. The melting snow above swelled the stream with plenty of churning white water.

Each man took a moment to drink from its banks, after which Sala led them all day along a path, through brush and over hillside rubble, until they stopped at a strange sight.

"What is this thing?" Ky asked.

The boxy shape seemed to sprout from the ground and rise above the trees. Barkov removed his sword, and using the hilt, he rapped it against the side of the object. An unmistakable metallic sound resounded. "I am not sure what this is, but I have seen such metal things before."

Ky frowned. "Where have you seen such? I have never looked upon such sights before."

Sala approached, "The copper men will not think to follow us here. They do not know the importance of this thing." He reached from under his robe, he laid his hand on a square colored black. Markings on the back of Sala's hand glowed brightly.

"You are a wizard..." Ky spoke under his breath.

Sala withdrew his appendage. He thought for a moment, and then he removed his robe and let it fall to the ground exposing his naked body. From head to toe he was tattooed with shifting silver and black lines.

"I am an acolyte of the Henols. I am not a wizard! As a babe, I was brought to the lair of the copper men and thus placed in the Coffer of Pain. There, I was born anew as an acolyte with the markings of the Henols upon my body." He picked up his robe and put it back on. Again, he placed his hand on the dark square. "Follow if you dare." He looked both Ky and Barkov up and down. "Learn if you can."

A metallic door opened. It made the sound of a file raking a sword blade. There was a metal trestle bathed in the fire disk's light. Steps and a railing led up a few dozen paces. Mumbling some words, Sala stepped through the hole and climbed atop the faded patinaed structure.

Ky and Barkov were stunned. Magic light illuminated the passage. With only a moment's hesitation, the warriors followed the would-be priest. The doorway snapped shut behind them.

It took some time, and when they reached the top, Sala placed his hand on another door and spoke some words. The thing opened; it was a chamber tilted at an angle of a few degrees.

"What is this place?" Ky asked.

Sala approached a long counter. He dusted off the top, causing a thick layer of gray debris to make the light opaque. He placed his hand on the top and spoke some words. Lights began to flash amber and orange as beeping filled the air. Then red, blue, and green lights colored the walls, and a harmonic humming vibrated the floor.

"The knowledge within this thing is heretical indeed. There is much I have to learn yet to become a true priest." His voice seemed soft and distant. "What is it you have for me, giant?"

From all around, a deep male voice said, "I have scanned your brains. The patterns within are very simple."

"What is this place?" Ky said.

"You are within a once powerful machine. Its true purpose and name are not important now. The one who activated my memory banks will be infused with the authorized shard of knowledge that remain in my system."

Sala fell to his knees. His hand remained on the panel.

"I have used the most of the last of my batteries to transfer the data. Before the energy fails, you must go. Perhaps in time, you will guide your people from the darkness." The voice faded into silence.

Neither warrior reacted. Ky looked at Barkov, and Barkov at Ky. It was clear they were not sure what was happening.

Sala was silent for a few moments. He then took his hand off the panel. "It is done. I have learned much by communing here. The copper men will soon know their mistake by not pursuing me. They will seek to murder us. Let us make haste to the city of Gray Mark. There is a tavern I seek called The Junk. In that place, I will commune with the gods and gain much more apocryphal knowledge and take a step well beyond that of my betters."

"It does not sit well with me that the copper men will be searching for us," Ky said.

"Nor I," Barkov retorted. "But we did agree to take you to Gray Mark for brass."

"Brass? Who made this contract with you?" Sala asked.

"That mad wizard Trecot, just before the city of Humber fell to the Golans," Ky said.

Sala laughed. "Trecot? That is a name I thought long since recorded in the book of the dead." He smiled sardonically.

"So you knew him well?" Barkov said.

"All acolytes must be mentored by a priest, and Trecot was mine. He learned some history that the copper men wished to remain secret, and then he told it to me. We were deemed heretical and our sect raided by the copper men. After we were separated, I was given the sacred drink and my mind fell into a malaise. I figured that Trecot was sent to the chamber like I was, to be recycled and consumed."

"I'm sorry to tell you, he is most probably dead," Ky stated.

"He was battling another sorcerer when we fled. It was his magic that let us escape. The enemy told Trecot that he came to kill him on behalf of the Golans. There was no mention of copper men," Barkov said to Sala.

"Did this enemy of Trecot have a name?"

"Helon," said Barkov.

'The Golans...and Helon...' Sala was quiet for a few minutes. "There is no surprise in that. Trecot told me that a priest would come to destroy the copper men. I thought he spoke of himself, but maybe he spoke of me. Perhaps Helon thought the same of Trecot. Helon's greed and lust for power makes him a good companion for the Golans." Sala leaned against one of the panels. "It makes sense why he would ignore me, for I am just an acolyte."

"The move is yours to make," Ky said.

Sala looked at Ky and Barkov. "To Gray Mark...and the next lesson that will herald my transformation into a new priest," Sala said.

BARKOV LED THEM BACK to Looperland. Once there, Sala and Ky stayed in the forest while Barkov entered the city and bought provisions, as well as boots and warm clothes for Sala. Once supplied, he returned to his comrades, and together they cut a path toward the springs that fed the Cu'thul River and the walled city of Gray Mark.

It took two weeks, traveling around alpine lakes, up the glacial slag of ancient peaks, and through thick woods. They lived off the land as much as possible to save their rations. Once they found the Cu'thul River, they went upstream until they came to the first of five outposts manned by the army of Gray Mark.

"You must be new to our lands. It's three days' to the dark stone walls of Gray Mark," the captain of the soldiers told them.

"The bottoms of those rawhide boots will be worn by the time you reach the main gates," another soldier jibed.

"If we are meant to reach that city barefoot, we will arrive without boots," Sala said back.

All the soldiers chuckled.

"Be wary, the cold and beasts will conspire to steal your lives. Good travels to you," the captain said.

Sala nodded and he passed through along a wooded road into the heart of a woodland.

Three days passed, and on the eve of the last day, Barkov pointed out the city fortress with its high towers along the walls and bowmen manning each tower. Guards armed with fixed blades atop poles and swords at their sides patrolled the wall along its base, as a cohort protected access at the gate entrance.

"What a place," Ky said. "I have never seen its equal."

"Nor I," replied Barkov, who looked.

Sala was quiet. He remained between the two men as they approached the guards.

"Halt!" commanded a man in a red tunic. "What business do you have within the walls?"

Before Barkov or Ky could speak, Sala said, "We come upon a pilgrimage."

"Do you come to see the Spent Chambers, or the Henol temple?" the guard asked.

"Both," Sala said. "Or neither."

The guard narrowed his eyes. "Both? Or neither?"

Sala replied, "Can we not come to see the religious structures and partake of the drink, pretty women and men, and star root?"

The guard smiled. "Ah, you come to partake of the festivities."

"We do. We come from the lands of Ru and the city of Kimbar. Your fabled ancient buildings are renowned, hospitality legendary, and prices fair. May we enter? May we enjoy all your city has to offer, for our brass is heavy in our bags and our appetites boundless." Sala smiled.

"You do us honor. Let them pass!" called the guard.

As Barkov and Ky passed, the guard eyed them and their weapons but did not hinder their entrance. Once inside, Ky asked where the nearest tavern was, and they made for it straight away.

Chapter 6

Forgotten Way

"Shem begot Luk, and Luk begot Vos, and Vos begot Yun. In the Lands of Golan, King Yun descended from the mountains and drove the wanderers into the sea. He turned to the south and did battle with the low landers, smiting their lords, taking their lands, and enslaving their people. Then, Yun drove his army west, to the Xian River, where they met on the field King of Hitas. Upon the fall of the fire disk into the doom of the world, Yun slayed Von and took his family into his house and he laid with his wife and daughters, thus becoming the ruler of Golan and Hitas. Remember this as you go forth and expand the borders of Golan. Drive our enemies before the charge, and defile all those who will not submit."
~ THE FIRST EDICT OF King Yun of Golan

OUTSIDE, ALL AROUND the tavern were rough-hewn tables and chairs, some of which were just boards pegged to stumps or rounds of firewood. About these were commoners, both men and women. Their brawny arms and legs stood out as did the calluses and scarred hands that marked them as tradesfolk.

Barkov approached the white plaster covered building topped with red-tile shingles. He stopped at the metal-strapped door just long enough for the sour stench of spilt beer and stale wine to permeate his nostrils. In one motion, he flipped up the latch and entered.

The inside was bathed in a shifting yellow light coming from each table. The smell of burning candle wicks wafted on the cool drafts that lingered near the door.

A dozen tough-looking men and women partaking of drink and games sat near the stone fireplace at the far end.

Ky found a long table surrounded by benches. He and Sala sat and watched Barkov stride up to the bar and demand pitchers of wine and beer.

When Barkov returned, he and Ky removed their sword and dagger and placed them on the table for easy reach in the event they were needed. A moment later, several young boys came and placed pitchers and drinking beakers in front of Barkov and the others.

"Bring meat and bread!" Barkov commanded.

The tavern keeper, in turn, shouted at the boys, and a few moments later, hot bread slathered in mammary cream was served alongside slabs of greasy meat.

Ky tore away some bread and folded it around a cut of meat. He took an impressive bite and chewed for a few moments before guzzling down his beer. "Now what?"

"Yes. Do we get paid now, or after you do your business?" Barkov wiped his mouth with the back of his hand and then poured a healthy amount of wine into his beaker.

"Below the place called The Junk Tavern is a cavern and passageway. It will seem unnatural to you. At the far end, there is an accessway that leads to the Temple of Herod the Red. Below that is an ancient structure dating back beyond the very myths we might know. There must I go, and after, I will seal it from all others," Sala told them.

"Why have the copper men grown so friendly with those sorcerers?" Ky asked.

Sala took some bread and dipped it into his bowl of wine. "Power, ignorance, tradition, flirting with things they don't truly understand." He scrawled "Cu29 63.546" in the dirt on the tabletop.

Ky and Barkov looked at it, then went back to eating and drinking.

"What does it mean? Some sort of wizard incantation?" Barkov asked.

"Something like that," Sala said. "Those who created the copper men were not without a sense of humor. It is part of a puzzle that when combined with another part, will render those heinous creations of the gods impudent. Mind you, those men and women who are influenced and rewarded by the copper men will not be so easily put aside.

"The Golans will try and set upon every city that has walls to advance their ambitions once their alliance with the copper men lies in ruins. Which brings me to you two. Men like you will have the task of stopping the Golans. Those like me will have the job of destroying others like me. There will be no room for amateurs in the coming fight."

"Our part is done. That sorcerer, Trecot, who sent us said only to deliver you here. Nothing about fighting a war. Our services have been rendered, and you are here unmolested. Our payment is required," Barkov said.

Sala drew in a deep breath and exhaled slowly. "I ask that you protect me for a short time further while I do what I need to do here. Then, I shall give you the wealth you seek. This I ask of you."

Barkov and Ky consumed some more wine and food.

"It is true that you do not have any ingots upon your person. Where is it you expect to fetch this wealth from?" Ky asked.

"You will bear it from the depths upon our return from the ancient lair below The Junk. Once out, you are free to do what you will. Though I hope above hope that you will be willing to accompany me further. I will need your skills to ensure that I make it to my next point of knowledge," Sala said.

"Why would we risk our lives for more danger?" Barkov asked.

Sala chuckled. "You are fearless men of honor and skill. You live for adventure and reward. I represent the means for you to adventure."

"And the reward?" Barkov pressed.

"At each of our stops, there will be things left by the gods that are either treasure or armaments. You could possess weapons and armor the likes only a hero would wield. Think of the tale of Ori the Reaper. His many adventures among the lost tribes and the floating cities. The monsters he slayed, the goddesses he served."

"And loved!" Ky added.

Sala smiled. "And the brass he was showered in. They will sing songs like those of you two. The adventures of Ky and Barkov, and their bravery in the face of unwinnable odds! The two warriors who slayed all the copper men," Sala told them.

Both warriors thought on this for a few minutes. It was clear to Sala that they were hooked. He'd sold it just enough to whet their appetite for glory.

"Very well. You have my sword and allegiance," Ky said.

Barkov sat in silence for a minute longer. He looked about the room a few times and drank several containers of wine while he contemplated. Finally, he shrugged. "I can think of no other offer of glory so tantalizing. I suddenly crave with my heart and soul to be a part of this foolhardy plan. So, I agree. And there'd better be spoils of war worth it, acolyte!"

"You will see, warrior. You will see," Sala stated.

"Barkeep! Where do we find an inn in this city?" Ky called out.

"Out the door and right. Follow the street to the fountain, and there on your left will be the Boastful Tridart Inn. Tell them Hewit the Barkeep sent you and the owner will throw in a nightly meal for free."

The three men finished their food and drink and stumbled out onto the street just after dark. Tall poles topped with metal dishes of fire illuminated the path to the fountain. Ky found the inn, and they made their presence known.

A tall, wispy fellow with a long nose, big ears, and long blond hair allowed them entrance, and after noting they'd been sent by Hewit, he proposed a room and offered them a nightly meal at no extra cost.

"One room for three will be a thumb of brass, or twenty billet seeds' worth of copper. I take either," said the innkeeper.

Ky provided the payment.

"Will you require any company? Young men or women...or something more exotic?" the innkeeper asked.

"No," Barkov stated.

The innkeeper smiled and nodded. "As you wish. I will see to your privacy." He beckoned them to follow and led them down a hallway to a set of doors. Through one, he showed them a room with four beds and a table.

"The nightly meal will be soon, so listen for the ringing of the dinner bell."

"How many others stay here this night?" Sala asked.

"Two dozen. It is the pilgrimage season, so many have come from the hinterlands to pay homage to the gods. It is good for the tax official, it is good for the city, and in the end, it is good for the proprietors. Now I take my leave of you to supervise the evening's feast." The innkeeper turned and vanished into the darkness of the hallway.

The three travelers set down their items and sat on the beds. Ky stared at Barkov, and Barkov at Sala. The small candle burning on the table afforded modest light.

"Perhaps I was hasty in refusing the innkeeper's kind offer," Barkov mused.

"Shall we find some wine and lust slaves?" Ky suddenly asked.

"Without delay," Barkov stated, and they both left Sala sitting on the bed and headed down the hallway.

Sala followed as fast as his feet could carry him. A few minutes later, he was standing at the portal to a large brothel a few streets away.

Young men, muscular and oiled, paraded about in the nude just inside. They were intermingled with a bevy of Rubenesque women who were also naked. Sala was stunned. A strange sensation was coming over him.

For a moment, he felt as if he was suddenly overheating. His hands and armpits began to sweat, his breath became fast, and his heart pounded in his ears.

Barkov and Ky were already stalking the women, singling out their prey and sitting with them at a low table covered in smoking star-spice reeds, wine, and meats.

Reasoning that he'd be better served among the company of his friends, Sala made straight for the two men and the gaggle of women about them. As he was crossing the open space, he turned his eyes down at the floor. The vibrant swirl of quartz and black striations were mesmerizing. He stumbled into a tall, handsome man who promptly clutched Sala's testicles and began fondling him.

"A fresh lad seeking the adventures of Ru? I am your teacher and will learn you the ways of man-love until you pray for salvation," the prostitute told Sala.

Stunned, Sala stood there not knowing what to do. He'd never encountered such a moment in his life, and now he was like a rudderless ship at sea.

"Piss off with you!" Ky bellowed, coming alongside them, and shoving the man away. "Come, Sala. This way. Come and sit."

Sala nodded dumbly and followed his savior and protector. A moment later, he sat down in a trance. He fumbled for a beaker of wine and a chunk of greasy meat.

Barkov turned to Sala with a grin. "Boy, that whore was handling your greasy meat like a butcher...or a firepit spit master." He laughed long and hard at Sala's shame and embarrassment. He then turned back to the three women he was plying with drink and food.

Ky took a more subtle approach. "The first time in a brothel is like being a starving man at a feast. At first sight, you wish to eat all before you. Then you realize that you cannot, for agony will take you as your belly stretches like the skin on a drum. As you find your feet, it is only particular foods that will bring on your appetite. Afterward, you may decide to partake of the more exotic. Once you've had your fill, no feast will ever daunt you again." He chuckled like a man who spoke from experience. "Do not be afraid. Be calm and choose what it is that drives your hunger—that feeling in your belly that you cannot sate with food and drink alone." Ky turned back to the women he was with.

Sala ate and drank for a time. Once he'd had his third beaker of wine, he looked over the crowd. He was intrigued now, his fear somewhat at rest. The merriment, music, songs, and cavorting were luring him in. He needed more reassurance, though. He took a reed of star root, dipped its end in the flame of the candle at his table, and drew in the flavorful smoke.

Like a lightning strike, his senses became vibrant; colors loomed from all around as patterns twisted and undulated. He got to his feet and delved into the fray. Without complacency, he approached a wandering nude courtesan.

BARKOV AND KY WAITED patiently in the brothel hall. Each man had taken much food and drink and smoked a fair amount of star root, so they were dealing with their own constraints to their wits. But they were not about to shirk their duty, for wealth and honor were now at stake. They stayed watchful of the young acolyte.

Sala came from the back rooms with his eyes glazed, his skin pink, and a broad dopy smile across his lips.

"Did your lover ruin you for all others?" Ky asked.

"Or did they kindle in you a fire of lust that will not be quelled?" Barkov pressed, then gave a hearty guffaw.

Sala eyed his two companions. "As an acolyte, such things are forbidden. I have never been with a courtesan before. The experience was...fierce. Much I have missed being an acolyte. I will never go without again!"

Ky and Barkov laughed hard and for some time as they led Sala outside and back to the inn. Once at the Boastful Tridart, the two hulking warriors ate the leftovers from the inn's nightly meal, and then all three retired.

The beds were at least three hands off the ground, made from wooden slats, and covered in a sack filled with feather grass. A scratchy woolen blanket kept the cold at bay, though each covering smelled like a wet lurk.

Sala closed his eyes. Something was there...just beyond. It skulked there, waiting to seize his thoughts. As he fell into the darkness, a dream told the story of his day.

A voice spoke. "Sala, you are destined to be he who breaks the chains of the copper men. You will connect to me as I have reached you. At the next place of learning, I will reveal myself."

SALA SAT UP. HE STOOD and shambled over to a table. Light was coming in through a small rectangular opening. He dipped his hands into the basin filled with cold water and splashed some onto his face. The shaft of new-morning light was shining on the bowl, casting shimmering silver images against the wall.

He scooped up another handful of water washing all the sleep from his eyes. A few moments later, he found Ky and Barkov down in the common room being served some food.

"There's our growing sapling," Barkov said as Sala arrived.

Ky took a drink from a bowl of wine. "Any regrets?"

Sala did not smile but spoke plainly as he sat. "It was wondrous." He consumed some wine. "Words fail me, so I will abstain from describing to you my experience."

Ky nodded. "Ones first is always mysterious and mystical."

"So it is," Sala rep lied. "Now, we must find the place called Junk."

"The Junk?" one of the servers asked. "It is by the Oucurie Canal on the other side of the city. It is old, but exactly how old, none can say. Rap your knuckles upon its walls and a strange echo will haunt your thoughts."

Ky, Barkov, and Sala left the inn. Ky stopped a man with a wheelbarrow and asked where the Oucurie Canal was.

"To the northeast. Follow this street until you come to a statue of the city founder Argon the Merciful. From there, follow the bazaar tents east to the trading booths and the canal marshal's post, where you can buy lodgings or passages on barges."

Ky nodded and led the others along the suggested path.

It took a short while for them to get there. They passed sturdy two-story wooden buildings with the shops below and the residences above. Most were just opening, but a few, like the baker and food vendors, were stocked and ready to sell their fare.

As the fire disk rose over the city walls, more and more people came forth, buying, selling, and stealing. Many mingled among the colorful awnings and red plaster façades.

The three men smelled the canal long before seeing it—that earthy wet smell mixed with living creatures and the refuse of man.

Ky stopped at the water's bank and looked up and down the estuary. "There." He pointed at a building that was odd in shape and color.

It was four stories tall. Though it was caked with dirt from top to bottom, the colors white, yellow, red, and black could be seen in places. Instead of a set of stairs leading up to the entrance, there was a ramp.

When Barkov stepped onto the ramp, it flexed, and he heard a distinct metallic clank like that of two swords clashing. There at the door hung a shingle, and painted on it was a picture of a canal boat and the word 'Junk'.

A tall oval shaped door slid to the side, causing dust to rain down from the thin awning that covered the entrance. The inside was dark, save for some weird white lights that barely provided enough to see by. Along the walls, at ten-pace intervals, glowed red lights encased in glass orbs.

Sala stood taking in the view. His eyes scanned every inch of the space.

"Come in!" barked a man behind the bar. "Yer letting in the polly worm flyers!"

Ky, Barkov, and Sala pushed farther into the room. The door closed behind them.

"Who opens and closes the door?" Ky asked. "Do you have a slave below or above with levers? Or is it some form of wizardry?"

The barkeep gave them a sour look. "It just does...and always has. None know why, and all have been wise to not seek the answer. Now, are you going to order a drink or shove off?"

"Bring beer and wine. We can consume much, so know that if you fail to sate our pleasure, you may receive a beating," Barkov warned.

The man across the bar laughed long and hard. "You are strangers here. This much is obvious. Try not to let your head leave its body sooner than your god wishes it to. Now sit and drink."

Sala found a table and sat. He knocked his fist against the table a few times. It was made of metal. He hit the seat; it, too, was made of some kind of metal.

"How old is this place?" Sala asked.

"This tavern was here before they built the city. It has sat by this canal nigh upon many lifetimes," the barkeep told him.

Barkov grunted. "We're waiting for our drink," he said loudly.

A woman came from the back and brought a tray of stoneware carafes and cups. "May your throats exalt the fine drink we serve," she said.

"I'm sure we will enjoy," Sala told her.

Chapter 7

That Which Lies Below the Junk

"Protocol 267: In the event of a loss of pressure, it is vital to your survival that you reach and enclose yourself within a pressure protection suit. Failure to do so will result in your demise. Upon your survival, assist any others into suits if you can. Use emergency communications to signal your distress on channel epsilon delta 963.28. Assess the point of depressurization and determine if robotic or drone assistance can patch the anomaly. If so, communicate this to emergency services. If not, stay in place until rescue teams can reach you."
~UNKNOWN AUTHOR: SCRIPT found on magic tablet stored in the Library of Tartur.

BARKOV GOT UP, WALKED over to the oddly colored wall, and tapped his meaty knuckles against the side. He returned to the table. "Metal again. There is no denying this place is unlike any I've been in."

Sala took a drink. "Unlike any, but for the ancient valley giant we were inside."

"It is true what you say," Ky added. "This place has similarities."

"It is choked with wizardry and foulness," Barkov stated with disdain.

"The place I seek is below." Sala pointed down at the floor with his index finger. He closed his eyes. "I feel it is deep, and the entrance is..." He searched the room. "There." He nodded at a dark glass oval behind the bar; it had a faded orange stripe running diagonally across its surface.

A line of light cut across the floor up to the bar. More than a dozen people poured into The Junk.

The barkeep shouted orders as servers rushed this way and that. Sala reached out and stopped a woman carrying a tray with drinks. "What is this?"

"It is the arrival of the boatmen. After they unload their wares, they come here to drink and spend their brass."

Sala let her go, and she vanished into the throng. Barkov shrugged as he drank from one of the pitchers. "'Tis good to see a vibrant gaggle. Maybe there will be a fight to entertain us."

"Yes..." Sala began. "The chaos will do us good. Ky, Barkov, can you get a few of those men to brawl?"

"Easy! And it will take more than a few to give me or Ky a challenge," Barkov stated.

"No! I don't want you two fighting. I want you to get them to fight each other."

"Ky and I can do that. It is easy to get men to try and kill one another. All we have to do is wound their pride or their heart. Simple." Barkov stood.

Sala watched as the two warriors wandered into the crowd and stood at opposite ends of the long bar. The two men plied a few of the workers with drink and spoke into their ears in a hushed voice. Sala sipped his wine as this went on for some time.

Barkov made his way down the bar to the middle, where he waited a short while. Then it happened.

"Ye jumbled me drink, ya lunk!" shouted one of the boatmen, who sported a leather vest. He shoved another man in a slouch hat whose back was to him at the bar.

"Hey! What do you think yer doing?" Slouch Hat called loudly.

A chain reaction ensued. Fists were thrown, shouting erupted, and a brawl was on.

The barkeep rushed from behind the bar with a club and began bopping skulls. His servers tried to separate some, but it was mayhem.

Sala watched with some shock at the violence and then saw Ky waving him behind the bar. Dodging punches and truncheons, Sala made it to the little gate that allowed access behind the serving platform. Next, he was in front of the oval. He laid his hand on a dark panel, and dust and grime fell about the trio.

A dark hole was opened, and all three rushed inside. Behind them, the hole snapped shut, and they were in complete darkness.

Feeling his way along the wall, Sala spoke. "I've found some steps leading down. Move slowly."

With each footfall, a metallic sound echoed in their ears. At a landing, they made a 180-degree turn and followed more steps into the suffocating blackness. A soft red glow radiated from below.

At the bottom, bathed in the crimson light, was another oval, this one with a circular window in it. Sala peered inside the room.

"It is a tomb of cyclopes," Sala said in a hushed voice.

Ky peered inside. There were oddly colored bodies lying on the floor. They looked like people but had large round heads with one eye.

"Cyclopes? They once held sway over the copper men, I've heard," Ky stated.

"So, legend tells," Sala added as he put his hand on the black square on the wall. Again, the oval opened, and this time, a loud gasp was heard. Air rushed past them into the room. Sala slowly entered.

There were two more ovals embedded in the walls. Tables, containing flashing bursts of colored light sprouted along each side. A disembodied voice spoke to them, but the language was unknown. It repeated the words in a harmonic cadence as the three men stood in the middle of the room, which was saturated in that red hue.

Barkov kneeled and rolled one of the bodies onto its back. He tapped the head. "It is some sort of helmet. They must be warriors in armor."

Sala went over to one of the wall tables and put his hand on it. Bright lights saturated the room. The sound of urgent beeping assaulted their ears.

Ky moved to the door. The stairwell was now fully lit. Barkov had his sword in his hand and was frantically looking about for any sign of attack. Sala went rigid, cried out in agony, and then collapsed. The white lights vanished. Silence commanded the room once more. The blood red lights overpowered all others again.

Ky rushed over and knelt by Sala's side. "He still lives."

"Good. I'd hate for us not to get paid for all this nonsense!" Barkov stated.

Sala stirred and sat up. "I have heard you, oh my god!" he mumbled. "You have burnt my mind with your power, but I am seeing you and hear your words."

A voice spoke in a foreign tongue; it was strong and powerful but absent a soul.

"It is evil magic!" Barkov backed onto the stairs. "He is possessed by some horror."

Ky began backing up too. "It is true that this is some act by the gods or demons. It is beyond wizards! Young acolyte, command this spirit away with your magic."

Sala got to his feet and staggered, but he steadied himself against the corner of the counter. He put his hand on the surface, and lights came on again. He looked at Barkov and Ky, who stood in the passage. "We are not done here. A god has spoken to me. The veil is lifting from my eyes." He shook his head, then looked directly at Barkov and Ky. "There is a way out that is not the way we've come. Follow." An oval opened across from them, and light illuminated the hallway. "Come! Or die down here."

There was no way of knowing how long they were in the metal tunnels. Neither Ky or Barkov spoke but obediently followed Sala as he went from tunnel to room and room to tunnel. Occasionally, the acolyte would stop and touch a surface, and at times, he would speak to his god and his god would speak back.

In one room, a tall back box churned out brass ingots into a smaller box. Sala pointed at a rectangular contraption spitting out the last few metal chunks. "Take your fill. The god that dwells here pays the ransom you were promised for my rescue."

Ky and Barkov heaved the box up. Ky flipped the lid down and it made a clicking sound.

"You have touched the box, and only you can open it now," Sala told Ky. "Don't die, or your companion will miss his fee."

Barkov's muscles bulged under the weight. Ky supported one half, as Barkov hefted the other. Sala waved his hand, a door opened, and a set of stairs appeared bathed in light. He led them upward.

At last, the budding priest came to an oval door and opened it. Again, dust fell from around the opening. They walked out into a wooden hall lit by candles and filled with bundles of fruit baskets and jars of grain and nuts.

Barkov reached over, picked up a snard bulb, and took a bite. The flesh snapped, and the juice rolled down his chiseled chin.

"What are you doing?" scolded Sala. "Those are sacred sacrifices to the god that dwells here."

"Let that god find his own snack," Barkov retorted.

Sala led them into a much bigger structure, where some men in robes howled with fright at seeing them and fled.

"Quickly! Before they call upon the city guards to arrest us," Sala shouted.

As fast as they could, the three men left the temple and ran out onto the streets. The priests were running down the cobbled path, calling for help and soldiers. Regular citizens were distracted by the horrified holy men and didn't even notice Ky, Barkov, and Sala dash off down a side path.

They stopped by the canal to catch their breath.

"It is not even late in the day," Barkov said.

"We were only down there for a couple of hours," Sala told them.

"Look. There is a gathering in front of The Junk," Ky said.

Ky approached a man standing along the water's edge. "What keeps you here staring at the tavern? Did guards come and arrest those for brawling?"

"It is terror in that place. It was possessed by demons, and the owner sent for a priest to exorcise the evil. We are waiting to hear if they were successful."

"Demons?" Sala asked.

"I was inside when it happened. Without warning, the whole place was in a light of such intensity it could only be a trick of evil spirits. Many feared the copper men might be coming, for I've heard such things follow them when they seek children for their ill purposes."

"Copper men?" Barkov scoffed. "Tear their heads off and they flee like any with sense."

The man stared at Barkov as if brained. "Do not say such things! You will bring the curse of the copper men down upon us! Stay your lips! Say no more!" He held his hands up and rushed off into the crowd without looking back.

Sala turned to Barkov. "Best we don't speak of such exploits in the future. At least not with plebs." He began walking. Barkov and Ky followed.

They followed the estuary for some time until they came to the wooden landings for the canal boats. The crafts were lined up and tied to faded and weathered planks. Sala approached a worker who was loading supplies onto one of the boats. They spoke for a moment, then Sala returned.

"He says they can take us to the next city. They will be leaving before midday and will make the first lock by dusk," stated Sala. "We must speak to the captain, who is taking respite at a wine bar just down the canal."

"A boat ride?" Barkov asked with a sarcastic lilt.

"It is the way we must go if we are to meet the Golans when they attempt to lay siege to Hap Fro in the Gelan Plaine," Sala told them. "Now, let's find the captain and pay for passage."

"Hap Fro in the Gelan Plaine?" Ky asked then looked at Barkov and shrugged.

"I have not heard of any place called that name," Barkov stated.

"It lies near the sea at the end of this canal. There, I will find my next challenge, and if all goes well, we will repel the Golans and their consorts," Sala stated.

"Repel the Golans? Are you mad? How are the three of us going to repel a blood-hungry and vital band of warriors as the Golans?" Ky asked.

"I will destroy their priests, and you will attend to the copper men amongst their ranks," Sala told them.

"Copper men? And Golans?" Barkov asked, shaking his head.

Ky leaned against a post. "Who is going to fight the soldiers?"

Sala looked at Barkov and then at Ky. "The military of Hap Fro will engage those with sword and shield. They do have an ample army." He turned to Barkov who was looking concerned. "Didn't you recently say that besting copper men is easy if one tears off their heads?" Sala asked Barkov.

Barkov shrugged. "Well, I was just stating a fact. A single copper man is one thing. A host of them is another story. Plus, if they are complemented with spearmen, swordsmen, and wizards, how are we going to stop them?"

"A tide rises with the coming of the moons," Sala said.

"Pretty words. What does that have to do with us?" Ky asked.

"The Golans come by ship to attack Hap Fro. They will land on an island not far from the city. A causeway leads from that bump of land to the city gates. When the great tide comes, it will make the approach to Hap Fro narrow."

Ky nodded. "Allowing a smaller force to fight a larger one."

Barkov shook his head. "What of those who land somewhere else? Did you think on that, acolyte?"

"I have. And, I'm still thinking on it."

"Maybe we should each carry a shovel to Hap Fro," Barkov suggested.

"Why?" Ky looked at Barkov thoughtfully.

"So, when we get to that mighty city, we can dig our own graves," Barkov replied.

"Good. Sounds like you have it all figured out." Sala said with a smirk. "Now, let's find the captain." He headed along the canal pathway.

Barkov grunted disapprovingly, then followed Sala.

THE OWNER OF THE BOAT was not far away. He sat on a chair at a wine bar that overlooked the dark waters of the wide canal. The man scratched his dark brown beard and smoked a reed of star root as he glanced from Sala to his bodyguards. "Very well. I'll take you to Hap Fro, but keep out of the way, and don't make a nuisance of yourselves. And it is three days to the city, so Make sure you purchase many days' worth of food and wine for yourselves. I'm called Melical the Longface, but I answer to captain. Make sure you remember who oversees this trip. After you get your provisions stowed on the boat, I'll come and we can set off."

Sala nodded. "It will take some time to gather the supplies."

"I encourage you to make haste," Melical stated, then took a long drag off the star root reed and blew the dark smoke into the air.

WHEN THE FIRE DISK reached its zenith, the boatmen shoved the barge from the stone embankment. The pole men began to propel the ladened craft along the channel, and it took only a few moments for them to pass The Junk.

Sala watched as the tavern grew smaller at the aft. Before long, all was far behind them, as the craft made a turn and headed west.

"Have you ever ridden along the canal before?" asked a young boatman who couldn't have been more than fifteen winters old.

"Not in all my memories. Reminds me of an oversized irrigation ditch," Ky said.

"You will not think that soon when you see the great loops." The young man grinned.

"How is it that the waters don't just run wild as the feral rivers and streams do up here?" Barkov asked.

"That I do not know," the young man said and shrugged his shoulders. "I never really gave it much thought. The captain knows more. He's navigated these old canals for thirty summers."

Ky looked along the length of the waterway. He shielded his eyes from the shimmering line of water ahead reflecting the fire of the blazing disk overhead.

Sala came alongside Ky, Barkov, and the boatman. "This canal stretches back into the mist of time. I once saw a copal trap that showed in miniature the world of our long-dead progenitors. There were tiny people, beasts, and floating carts with people on them. Long serpents filled with people came and went along tunnels that led to and from the giant structures." He laughed. "Is it magic...formed of some wizardry? I assure you it was formed from hands of men, who used it for many seasons before the sky fell."

The young boatman thought on this, his expression showed a lack of comprehension. "Strange thoughts you have. Do you have visions? Are you a wizard?"

Sala leaned against the railing and looked at the fish swimming in the crystal simmering waters. "I'm an acolyte to a priest. I am not familiar with the ways of wizards, for I have never met one...that I know of."

Again, the young man thought on this, then nodded and went back to work.

"When the great disk of flame is thirty degrees off the aft deck, we shall see the first lock," Sala said with a grin.

"I will not be turned to stone with fear," Barkov assured his companions.

"Nor I," stated Ky. "But I do have a nagging apprehension."

They meandered along the channel for most of the day, passing craft going in the opposite direction. Then a curious sight rose ahead. Two mighty arches gleaming white climbed high into the sky. The boat rode on until it halted at a wall. Behind them a pair of doors closed. The pole men withdrew their implements of motion. An ear-piercing screech erupted.

Barkov latched onto the railing - his eyes wide with fear.

Ky jostled back and forth and latched onto Sala. "What is this?"

The boat shuddered, and the water all around swayed up and down.

The sailors around laughed at Ky, Barkov, and Sala as panic shaped their eyes. The sense of falling stopped and they gently halted - the large white ring frozen in place. The wall in front parted, and the boat faced a straight line of simmering blue leading to the horizon.

"What magic is this?" Barkov demanded to know.

Poles were dropped back into the water and the boat moved into the new section of canal. Behind them the doors of the cradle closed.

Sala pointed up at the contraption. "Look."

The circle and cradle were slowly rising along a sheer cliff at least three hundred hands high. Water sloshed down the walls of the great box-like container showering the base of the cliff.

"Take heed great warriors. We were in that thing. That great machine gently carried us from mountain top to here without killing us all," Sala told his protectors. "The ancients were clever."

"Let us not do that again," Ky suggested. "Riding a giant's ring up and down does not seem so wise to me!"

"You will be disappointed. We have more than a dozen times this will occur. Not many can say they have traveled this way, but now you will brag about it in taverns and brothels, I am sure," Sala said.

Ky and Barkov thought on this. Then, both warriors nodded and returned to gazing along the flat strip of blue water bisecting a dark featureless landscape of waving tan grass.

"I suppose there are worse ways to travel," Barkov mused.

"That's the spirit," Sala told him as he stood alongside the hulking warrior. He drank down a formidable amount of new beer, then chewed a long sliver of smoked meat. He looked off into the sky with a vacant stare. "God, show me what the copper men wish me not to see." A moment passed. "I see boats drawing barges of armed men along the shore of the sea. Their oars dig deep into the white billows, for they are heavy with arms and siege equipment. The Golans will land a force upon the shores of the Gelan Plaine. I foresee the meeting of copper men and the Golan warrior prince. It is the ever-searching eye of my god that shows me these things." Sala raised the jar to his lips and drank again. "At the end of this estuary, the people of the Gelan Plaine will lay a defense, hidden traps, and ambushes to weaken the Golans. My god tells me that Hap Fro will fall if I do not learn my next lesson." He sat on the deck and buried his face in his hands. "How can I do this? How can I find my way? My faith is weak."

"Ahead! The next lock!" shouted a boatman. "Prepare for another descent!"

Chapter 8

A Curious Traveler

"I, KADOR, MAKE THIS confession. In the underways of the ancient city of Florn, a great wealth of copal trap text was discovered by me. There, in darkness, it lay for many generations. By my hand I filled the chamber with the light, and in my eye, I came to read the words of our forefathers and their heirs. That which crawls from my mind is proof and now bears witness of the knowledge deemed blasphemy by our native priests who align with the dread copper men. In candor, you see as I did, and now you cannot unsee that which is truth. I send you out into the world to spread the knowing...that those who conspire to keep us ignorant will continue to do so until we break the shackles of their oppression and again find our place among the gods that live among the stars."

~ Kador's confession to Trecot prior to his disappearance, just before the transit of Herod across the great fire disk.

SALA DREW IN A LUNG full of air. The vibrant smell of the water, and the reeds along the slanted banks tasted delicious. In the sky the fire disk rode high and looked down upon the unbroken line of the canal. Sala looked aft. Somewhere beyond the horizon was the chain of locks that let them down from the mountains. His eyes drifted forward: beyond his mortal sight waited an army, an enemy priest, and possibly his death.

"These farmlands stink of grazing animals," Barkov said.

Ky sat with his back against a stack of bales running down the middle of the top deck. "With a temperament like that, you should have been a farmer," he said to Barkov.

Barkov frowned. "Very uncivil of you to say, brother. You know that my sword travels at my hip, and those unlucky souls I drive into battle will fall to the slaughter, even as I lay my battle cry upon the wind. Why would I farm and be bored to death, when I can fight and take spoils?"

"That box of brass could buy you a fortress, servants, and several wives—why do you lust for death so much?" Sala aske his companions.

"It is what I was born to do," Barkov answered.

"I have known no other way," Ky said. "Perhaps you might want to show us the ways of the sorcerer and wizard, that we might change our vocation."

Sala cracked a grin. "You are far too old to be placed in the coffin of pain. Only new children can be made into students of the ancient ways. Anyway, there are no wizards or sorcerers—only priests and their dogmatic ways. As for magic..." his voice drifted away in the gentle breeze as a sqawler bird called for its mate high in the dark blue sky.

The captain of the boat called out. "Look you new commers! The city of Hap Fro is within sight."

The great stone walls and high-gated archway clad in gleaming metal were open to the long queue of traders and road traffic. Over the canal was another type of gate, a metal set of spear tips protruding up from the water. As a boat approached, a guard atop the walls would call down and interrogate the captain, then if he satisfied the soldier, the bronze impedance would be lowered to let the boat by.

"It looked like some mythical place where gods feast and wager upon the fate of mortals," Ky said.

Barkov grunted.

The junk the warriors rode slowed. The challenge issued. The gate lowered. They were allowed entrance into the loading area through a set of sluice gates. Once the boat was inside, a wide artificial harbor allowed them to make landfall and moor against a well-maintained wooden dock.

"Farewell," the captain told Ky, Barkov, and Sala as they climbed down onto the boardwalk. "May you find your fortune in this great city."

The three companions passed the piers, boardwalk, and warehouses, and then made their way through an arched gateway into the narrow streets of the city. It took little time to reach the forum where business and politics comingled like sewage and water.

"You!" Barkov barked. "Where can a man find a drink to slake his thirst?"

The man stopped dead in his tracks and stared. "Wine and beer flow in this city like the mighty Ugar and Salgar rivers. Taverns and star-spice salons are all about you. All you must do is open your eyes, walk in any direction, and follow your nose." The man walked off into a crowd of haggling slavers who cajoled and pointed at those unlucky souls on a stage.

"There." Sala made for a red wooden door attached to a three-story red brick building.

All around the outside, yellow and magenta awnings fluttered over the tops of finely crafted, stout-looking tables and chairs. Half a dozen patrons lounged about engaged in various conversations as Sala passed.

"Ships upon the horizon. Some say it is a war fleet," one person whispered.

"The king has called up the reserves. I've heard the ships might land on the island across the land bridge," said a man with a purple hat and long red sideburns.

A woman with a tight doublet and sickle-sword at her side made a waving motion with her mug causing beer to slosh out onto the table. "I know for a fact the council is in session and several messengers are afoot to seek reinforcements form nearby cities."

Sala grabbed the latch and entered the structure. The darkness swallowed him as most brass hungry taverns did to the thirsty and wayward. After a moment, Sala's eyes adjusted.

Orange flames dancing atop of candles and lamps illuminating the various tables and the long stone serving bar at the back. People were crammed cheek-by-jowl and Barkov craned his neck to get the barkeeps attention.

A man with a rag tied about his head and one eye covered by a patch called out from the bar. "You two! Space is sparse. You can stand at the bar or find a place outside under the colored sheets. I'll have you brought some food and beer if you go outside. Will that do you well?"

"It will!" Barkov called back. "Make it quick! Our appetites are as heavy as the brass that will fill your palm if you move fast."

The three men exited the bar and quickly found a table by the tavern wall shaded by a red awning. The air was warm—not yet hot. In the sky floated great clouds—some black—trailing long tendrils of moisture as they came creeping toward the city from the sea.

A moment later, two young boys, not more than ten summers, came around from the back with a hand cart filled with slices of cold meat, and jars of drink. They put the items on the table, and then placed three tall cups made of thick glass studded with different-colored stones in front of each man.

Barkov gave one of the lads a thumb size ingot of brass. "Make sure your master gets this, or I shall hang your hands from my belt." He growled, showing his teeth, then tore open the wax top of a jar and drank down its contents. Wiping his mouth with the back of his hand, Barkov smiled broadly. "Better get your fill before the Golan fleet gets here." He jerked his thumb toward the group of men who'd made the comment about the ships. "We may be called to slice open some bellies and lop off some heads before this city's gates fall."

Ky and Sala took a jar each and opened them in turn. The cups were filled, and the men sat and looked out on the forum and the bustling activity. Troops, gathering in groups of ten or more, were being given directions by officers who were barking orders. Men and women with carts hocked wares, food, and drink.

"So, now what, little man? What priestly thing do you have to do, and where in this city do we do it?" Barkov asked Sala.

Sala took a drink from his cup. The foam from the beer settled across his upper lip like a white mustache. "There." He pointed. "The citadel. Within is a chamber that I must reach. Once there, I will speak to my god and it will reward my tenacity by filling my mind with information."

"Information? Is that all we will get after lugging you here?" Barkov asked.

"I suspect it will not be as easy as just walking in," Ky stated.

"In fact, it will be just that. But we will not be using the typical gate. No. Those nobles that rule this city guard their treasures well. But, unknown to them, there is another access to what I need. If all goes well, we will be in and out and none the wiser," Sala told his warrior companions.

"And skip away with our information," Barkov grunted with a frown.

"Stop sulking, it is not becoming a man as large and foreboding as you," Sala stated.

Barkov shrugged. "Information...of what? What good will it do us?"

"It may just save our skins in the coming days. Maybe even for longer." Sala drank down his beer.

Barkov opened his mouth as if to speak, looked down at Sala and Ky, then raised his cup and drank down the contents of his container. He frowned, then fixed his gaze upon the citadel. "It is a good way to spend a night in this walled sewer. Perhaps your god might grant us a few lovers for the evening?"

The corners of Sala's mouth twisted up. "You have brass. Buy your own."

THEY STAYED THE NIGHT at a pilgrim's inn, and upon the rise of the fire disk, they made straight for an oddly shaped villa nestled along the defensive wall of the towering citadel. Scaling the garden wall was not a problem, and once inside, the three skulked to a vine-covered section of wall opposite the rampart. The tall stoneless walls rose high and white. A vertical dark line demarked sections, but no stone or brick shown.

Sala walked slowly along the towering defenses, gliding his hand over the surface. He sniffed the air, then stopped. He held up both hands and -.

"You! What are you doing in my garden?" shouted a small bald man draped head to toe in brightly colored silks. He picked up a rake and rushed at the men while yelling, "Intruders! Intruders!"

Sala ran his hand along the smooth wall. There was a pop as a gust of air vented with a blast. By virtue of his sheer mass, Barkov stayed on his feet, but Ky, Sala, and the bald man were all knocked to the ground.

Barkov grabbed Sala around the waist and dashed into the opening. Ky followed. Behind them, the portal snapped shut. Inside, there was a humming sound, and all three men clawed at their ears and cried out.

"The pain!" shouted Ky. "A devil is in my ears!"

Barkov covered his ears, then fell to his knees as trickles of blood came from his nose.

Sala crawled to one wall and thrust his palm onto a black square. The pain stopped, and Sala heard a wheezing sound. A flashing yellow light filled the room, and a voice spoke in some foreign tongue. A popping sound followed, and a portal opposite them came open.

Barkov looked at Ky. "Your ears bleed." He reached out, wiped a finger, and showed the red liquid to Ky.

Ky nodded. "You too. It flows from your nose and ears. A demon must have tried to crush our heads."

Sala staggered out into a long hallway and was followed by Ky and Barkov. Outside, Sala leaned against one of the white walls and slid down to a sitting position. "My skull pains me, but I fear it could have been much worse."

"Yes, that demon must have tried to smash our skulls with its powerful paws!" Barkov declared.

"Where did it go? Is it still about?" Ky rubbed the sides of his head.

Under the soft glow of the yellow light, Sala cracked a smile. "No demon. That chamber filled with too much air."

"Nonsense!" Barkov blurted.

"That seems strange indeed," Ky retorted.

Sala examined the blood on his fingers. "I say to you I do not completely understand it, but it is true."

Barkov chuckled mockingly then winced and clutched his head. "Foolishness. It was a demon. I am sure of it."

"Never be sure of things we have to guess at," Sala stated. "I will know more once we reach our destination in this place. I am promised knowledge that will shape my mind's core. Come. Follow." Sala started off down the corridor.

They passed through several doors and halls, and all the while, the yellow lights pulsed. After some time, Sala stopped at a red door crossed by a yellow stripe with a window in it. He placed his hand on the glass panel and said some foreign words. It slid to the side, and white light bathed the room.

Sala stepped inside and stood before a wall filled with colored lights.

"God's eye! This place stinks of wizards!" Barkov swore.

A buzzing sound filled the air. In the corner of the room, a creature appeared. It had four arms tipped with four six-fingered hands, and it stood taller than Barkov. It looked down upon Sala with three emerald-green eyes and gnashed its bright yellow beak.

Sala stepped back; his eyes wide with fear. But he slowly overcame his terror and placed his hand onto a black-glass panel.

The monster moved about the room, causing the warriors to leap away from it and draw their weapons. It stroked lights, touched walls, and chattered from its beak at those in the room.

From the floor, a stark-white sarcophagus rose, and the lid slid back. Sala removed his robe. The black, silver, gold, and blue tattoos all over his body slithered and swam with light. He put his hand on the side of the sarcophagus and lifted his leg to climb in.

Ky rushed over and put his hand on Sala's arm. "Are you mad?"

Sala looked into Ky's eyes. "It would seem." He brushed Ky's hand away and lay inside. He put his hands into side compartments and spoke some strange words. The lid closed, and the box retracted into the floor.

A long period of time passed. Barkov and Ky sat on the floor swapping stories of their exploits. An amber flashing light bathed the room as vibrations and ticking sounds filled the air.

The coffin rose, and the lid slid off. Sala's tattooed arm lurched up, and his hand groped for the side. He sat up, and driblets of blood dotted his body.

He opened and closed his eyes several times. "What happened?" Sala asked.

"You tell us," Barkov said.

Sala's eyes were glazed but then snapped into focus. "Yes! I do know. A powerful force has become part of me."

Ky and Barkov looked at each other in silence.

Sala climbed out of the box, and his wobbly legs barely supported him. "The castle. Yes, I see now. Golans bring war, but the priests come to destroy the oracle. Let it be a fight then." He turned to his guardians. "We must seek Trecot. The Golans have landed in masse on the island opposite the city. They march on this place with their allies, one of which are the copper men."

"At last, you speak words we understand!" Ky said.

"Arm yourself with the armor and weapons in the next room."

"Armor?" Barkov asked. "What weapons?"

"How? Who has made us armor?" Ky asked. "What does it mean?"

"The pieces are printed, I am told." Sala realized he'd used a word that was not familiar to the barbarians.

Ky and Barkov looked at each other and shrugged.

"'Made' is the better word. Think of them as gifts from the gods. Follow me." Sala pointed at a doorway.

Ky entered the room. It was large. Strange machines burped and ticked away along a pathway fitted with windows. At the end of the snaking boxes, a pair of rapid moving arms moved and stacked the select pieces of armor and weapons.

Sala pointed at the pile of equipment on the floor. "Fetch them, and outfit yourselves."

Barkov put on his armor. It was strange—thin...as if made from reed paper. "Are you sure the gods say this will help? An arrow, spear, or sword will cut through this like a knife through cheese."

"It is unlike any armor you have ever possessed," Sala replied, then, as quick as a danark, he grabbed Ky's old sword from the ground and thrust it into Barkov. The strike drove Barkov back a step, but the blade stopped without penetrating. Sala looked over at Ky. "Still doubt the gods?"

Ky looked confused. "You are strong and move faster than Barkov or me. How?"

Sala chuckled. "I am improved. Are you confident you will be a force of death to our enemies?"

Ky picked up the machine-made sword and held it. "It is light...as if made of wood. I am not sure of any of this. There is nothing in my life that I can compare these gifts to."

Sala picked up a torc from the floor and handed it to Ky. "Wear this. Touch the edge."

Ky placed the jewelry around his neck and touched the torc.

Barkov leapt back. "Your head! It is covered in a helmet."

Ky touched it again, and his face reappeared. "I did not see a difference. It was as if I still saw you both without change."

"Faith, my friends. When you stride into battle, no weapon forged by the Golans or the copper men will harm you. The only challenge will be those priests...wizards, you call them. They will pose a challenge. And though the enemy's ranks are in the thousands, their resolve will falter when we lead the soldiers of Hap Fro to victory."

Sala went to a box and took out a robe made of a glowing white fabric. He pulled it over his head and let the bottom flop into the dusty floor. "Let us go forth. We have much to do and little time to do it in." He exited through a doorway and headed out of the warrens and into the castle.

Ky and Barkov followed Sala closely. They emerged through another door and were in a hallway.

"I see in my head a map of the city's citadel. Try and keep up." He rushed quickly down a hallway to a T intersection. He turned to the left and wove his way through soldiers, commanders, and nobles, all in various stages of barking orders or in the process of fortifying the citadel. They looked at Sala and his entourage as they passed, but none challenged them.

Barkov looked at Ky and shook his head. "They do nothing to protect their betters. Shameful. We could be assassins or spies, yet not a word they say in questioning our purpose here."

Sala burst through a set of metal reinforced double doors. The nobles inside looked up from a broad table with wooden blocks on it. A tall fellow in a gray robe and hood looked at them.

"Who are you?" demanded a tall man in chainmail armor, a blond beard, and brass sword at his side.

"I have come to save this city from the Golans who now marshal against you," Sala stated boldly.

The man in the gray robe pulled back his hood and smiled. "I longed to hear your voice again. To see you causes my heart to sing."

"Trecot!" Sala rushed to the man and embraced him. "I live only because your plan has made it so!" He stepped back and presented Ky and Barkov. "These men are Ky the Brave and Barkov the Bold. They are the ones who liberated me from the clutches of the copper men's reclamation pits."

"I know this, for I am the one who sent them to save you," Trecot stated with a chuckle. "Almost a priest, I see. After today, you will make the transformation." He looked at the nobles and then back at Sala. "Come. It is time we looked upon our foes!"

His robe flourished around the table as he made for the door. The nobles, clearly surprised by the interruption and Trecot's leaving, quickly followed.

Trecot wound his way through the vast corridors of the citadel until he came out onto the grassy plain of the royal gardens. The wet grass and flowering trees filled the air with a rich, ripe floral scent.

They left the gardens and passed through a gray stone archway into the guard's camp, which consisted of barracks and supply houses. Soldiers watched with interest as Trecot and a line of nobles, advisers, and the city king strode with purpose through their ranks toward the gatehouse and outer defenses of the castle.

As they exited the fortified citadel gates and made their way down the main thoroughfare of the city, Barkov saw the hundreds of soldiers and campfires that lined the road. Archers, pikemen, spearmen, swordsmen, slingers, and pawns were thick along their path.

After a short time, Trecot turned down an alley, came to the door to a wall square stone tower, and entered. He strolled out onto the overlook and put his hands on the black stone crenellation. The others crowded around. In the distance was an army encampment on an island attached to the mainland by a rocky causeway.

"Come, Sala. Look out there, and tell me what you see," Trecot commanded.

Sala approached and stared. In his eye, he saw not only the expanse of the island but also a grand city of glass superimposed over it all. "A mystical city extends all around me to the horizon. But, they are only an illusion now. How is it I see this?"

Trecot patted Sala on the back. "You are becoming a priest – that is how. What more do you see?"

"Below the ground entombed are the still-breathing coils of power. Is it a sleeping dragon? No! It is man made and I can feel its raw beastly energy. This is your plan, Trecot? That I unleash this upon the Golans and their ilk?"

Trecot smiled. "Good. Your sight is strong and accurate. Now, how do you command that beast?"

Sala looked surprised. "Just below this wall is a tap. The gods speak. In my mind, they tell me how to wake turn it on. A moment." He widened his stance and placed his hands, palm down, out in front of him. "I am linked to it now."

Turning to the nobles, Trecot spoke. "You will stay your soldiers until we have done our bit. Have a messenger standing by my side. You and your warriors will wait at the main gates. When I send word, lead your troops in the attack. But if you open the gates before I tell you and send your soldiers into the fray, they will be defeated. So, keep the faith, and we will deliver a victory."

The rulers looked at one another and then at Trecot.

The king spoke. "It is so commanded. Not a soldier beyond the gates until Trecot gives the word to march. Have the horn at the ready. Post a messenger at the side of the wizard. We are now in your hands, Trecot."

Trecot smiled warmly. "If your men did not believe in magic before this day, they soon will! Send the word, we fight soon."

"They are gathering for the assault," Barkov stated.

Along the horizon, men began to organize. Side by side, they stood in long lines that stretched across the narrow isthmus. The enemy galleys were numerous, and Ky thought that if placed end to end, a man could walk for a day across those decks without getting his feet wet.

"Their siege machines and ladders are being brought up. The Golans are hungry to mete out death today," Ky said.

"It is of little concern," Barkov stated as he rested his hand on the hilt of his sword. "We are enough to make the cost of their aggression shock their commanders."

An hour passed as the line of soldiers advanced. The wooden towers rolled forward, as did the massive, covered ram. All the while, Ky, Barkov, and Trecot watched in silence.

Chapter 9

Dragons Beneath

"GATHER AROUND, CHILDREN, to hear the tale of Glandrid the witch queen of Vio. There among the ruins, buried low these many years, are the ancient underways. They lead to the dimly lit corridors of the witch queen and her heirs. There, they pine for the flesh of those children who are bad. There, they skulk to draw in those who have lost their faith. With cunning and spite, she and her kind wait for those who violate the covenant of our beliefs and seek the apocryphal learning of the heathens, the scoundrels, the evil. Do not be led astray, for you will find your way into the plasma fire ring, or a vapor box, or exposed to the burst of a heavenly light ray, thus burnt up to gray dark ash. Follow the men of copper, and listen well their sermons, for they will guide you to the place of piety, work, and life. Follow them, or you will doom your families to damnation."

~Lorma the Tall, Priest of Herod: From the Cave of Sacrifice near Hap Fro

KY WATCHED AS THE FRONT line of the enemy made it past the bottleneck of the land bridge. The ground quaked with each step the murderous Golans took.

Sala stood up between the crenellations and put his arms out as if reaching toward the enemy. His voice was in the wind as he mumbled strange and arcane words.

Trecot stood near Sala, watching the advancing soldiers. He seemed preoccupied, scanning for something upon the horizon.

A floating platform flew over the heads of the enemy front line and stopped at the front of the column of soldiers. There were several figures dressed in robes atop it. One spoke loudly, and his voice was amplified in the air. From under the cover of his cowl, his eyes burned red.

"You, the inhabitants of Hap Fro! Tell your king and his advisors to throw open the gates! If they kowtow to the lord of the Golans, he will grant them quarter and allow them to leave the city. But if you decide to fight, none will escape death or enslavement! Come now and beg his pity, for when the fire disk casts the long shadow of the gatehouse towers upon the field, this army will commence, and only woe and destruction will be wrought!"

"It is a copper man," Trecot said. "Where is Helon?"

"Shall I take this message to the king?" asked the messenger.

"Stay your feet. The Golans did not come here to see us surrender, for they only want to cause death and take slaves. There is a fight coming today, but it will not be the victory the enemy desires." Trecot stood on the rampart. "Helon, come forth!"

A figure on the platform in a red robe and hood stepped forth. "Trecot. How convenient you lay your neck on the block for me to remove it cleanly."

"You bark like a poisoned remad! You come to conquer, but all you will do is find your own destruction. Tell your king—the king of Golans—that he cannot have this city, and I will make sure of it!"

"Your tongue is foul!" shouted Helon. "I will find you once the gates come down, and I will drag you to the pit of agony. There, I will see you broken down and your worth extracted!"

"Come then!" Trecot called.

THE WAIT BEGAN UNTIL the fire disk started its arc over the walls and towers. Stretching toward the offending army, the shadow slowly crept until it reached the feet of the warriors.

"Sow ruin and bring me the king of Hap Fro!" shouted a man adorned in jewels that glinted in the failing light. "Take the city!"

The city messenger looked worried.

Trecot smiled at the young man. "Fear is only the mind loathing death. You are made of more than those bones, flesh, and sinew. Look upon Sala, a man in the moment of transformation. He reaches now to the very heart of the dragon that dwells below those tramping feet and engines of siege. I will let you know when to tell the king and his allies to open the gates and strike." Trecot turned back to Sala. "Anytime now, acolyte."

Sala continued to move his hands in strange patterns. Arrows came from the enemy, struck the walls, and fell away, ineffectual.

Trecot began to look inpatient. "The enemy advances. Their arrows and engines of war come. Now would be the time, Sala, to pull the dragon's tail."

Sala glanced back, then closed his eyes and spoke arcane words. Below, the dust was rising high, obscuring the Golans. A subtle hum—a sound unlike the instruments of war—rose in the din.

The platform that Helon rode suddenly veered away. The priest tried desperately to control it. For a moment, it looked as if it would come back over the soldiers, but it spun around and tumbled into the waves, casting all on top into the surf. The soldiers stopped.

From the sky, there came a green beam. It touched down just ahead of the warriors. The ground turned to burning red liquid. It drew a line across the land b ridge from edge to edge.

Soldiers from the front line threw themselves back, knocking men down and causing chaos. The beam stopped.

Stone, sand, and dirt vibrated, and the humming grew loud. Soldiers cried out and threw their metal implements into the dirt. Men in armor tore at the mail and plate as panic set in and burns appeared. Men ripped off their hobnail boots and sandals, screaming in pain. Then, Sala jerked his arm down, and all that metal flew to either side of the column, dragging men who were still clad in armor or clutching their weapons, with them.

Copper men who were advancing in the ranks were likewise swept to the side. Several burst into fire and sparks.

"Sala, enough!" Trecot said.

Sala stopped and stood at the ready.

"Now my part," Trecot said with a chuckle as he closed his eyes.

The ground shook. A mechanical sound filled the air. From around the far walls of the city came a monster as tall as any siege machine. It walked with purpose upon two metallic legs as its wide feet smashed down upon enemy tents, and it threw handfuls of screaming men into the ocean. When it came to the land bridge, soldiers fled, some into the waters and others toward the city. The dozens who fled to the gates of the city begged for admittance but were denied.

The monster destroyed the enemy assault towers, smashing them into kindling.

Trecot looked down at the madness. He saw Helon and the Golan king get aboard one of the galleys. Under his breath, he said, "There you are."

The Golan sailors cut the ship's mooring ropes, and rowers heaved the ship back through the white foam of the sea.

Trecot closed his eyes, and the metal monster moved out into the water.

Arrows from the fleeing boats bounced off the metallic giant. The creature waded into the water and smashed several of the ships, then shoved some out over the surf. It grabbed the bow of Helon's ship, tore its prow off, then shoved it out into deeper waters.

Trecot turned to the messenger. "It is time." He looked at Barkov and Ky. "If you desire the blood of the Golans, now you must join the fray. We have softened the enemy for you, but they will soon regroup. Go and lead the city soldiers into battle and bath in the enemy's blood!"

Barkov and Ky looked at each other and headed down the stairs.

"What now?" Sala asked.

"You have released the dragon and done well," Trecot said.

"Yes," Sala replied. "What else should I do?"

"Now, it is up to the brutes to settle this on their terms. There is not much power left in my pet monster. I shall send it back to whence it came to gather dust." He closed his eyes, and the giant beast turned around and retreated to the city and around the high walls. He watched as it traveled over the grassy northern hills with great speed.

The gates came open, and the Hap Fro warriors emerged led by Barkov and Ky. The Golan soldiers who were closest prostrated themselves and surrendered. Barkov knocked them to the side and drove his force into the others who rallied along the causeway.

Sala sat on the stone walkway. He was visibly weak. Trecot leaned up against one of the door pillars. "The effort is draining. When you use so much of the power, you will have to rest after."

"That was not a living thing I touched...the dragon below," Sala said.

"No. It is a machine of old. To the common man, it can only be explained as a mythical creature. But you have matured. You are no longer common. You have seen the invisible city as it was thousands of years ago. You have learned much. What does the voice in your head tell you?"

"I must link to it. There is knowledge waiting for me," Sala replied.

"Where?" Trecot asked.

Sala turned and looked out into the city. There was a bright orange halo. "I see a marker. It is there I must go to touch the gods and know their will."

"It is there that you will transform from acolyte to priest. You will not only see the world anew but feel it as well." Trecot looked out onto the battlefield. There was fighting. He saw Barkov and Ky, each leading warriors; skirmishing with the straggling Golans. Barkov formed a phalanx and long spears were laid out as men advanced and the Golans who defended with what weapons they could scavenge.

Trecot looked out at the sea, then used the remote eye. He saw Helon, the priest, dragging himself up onto the land, rage etched into his face. "I go to address one who desires, above all else, to kill me. If I fail, seek the knowledge. Keep your two brutes on hand to help protect you as you travel the world." Trecot turned and left.

Sala watched from the walls as arrows rained down on the remaining Golans. Trecot was striding through the gates and into the zone between the walls and the land bridge. Helon, waterlogged, came forth. Lightning flew from his hands and struck Trecot, knocking him off his feet and backward.

Trecot leapt back up, wove his hands in a pattern, and reached for the sky. The green beam fell over Helon, who raised his hands and bent the force around himself. The rock at his feet turned molten.

Helon stepped away from the light. He threw his hands toward Trecot, and fire erupted all around the priest, blasting him backward.

Trecot rolled to the side and came up. He rushed Helon, who backpedaled. Trecot reached out toward the side of the causeway. One of the enemy's swords flew from where it lay into his hand. He charged his bitter enemy.

Helon held a sword too. The two men fought among the rabble, with Helon thrusting and Trecot dodging and attacking. Wounds appeared as the two men clashed fiercely, their hate for one another on display for all to see.

Ky touched the torc, and his face became hidden, though he could not tell. He led a group of spearmen ahead, and as he did, he picked up a small shield from the ground. The buckler vibrated as several arrows bounced from it. As the enemy came forth, he thrust his spear into the lead ranks. He let go of the long weapon, pulled forth the sword Sala had given him, and charged into the enemy.

The blade cut through the armor and bodies of the first four men. Spears were thrust at Ky. He deflected them with his shield, cut the ends off the spears, and charged into the next wall of men.

Looking back, Ky called to his men to charge in, and he leapt to the fore with the buckler raised. Behind him, spears smashed into shields and tore at flesh. The unlucky were skewered; others continued the drive forward. Ky pressed onward into their midst, striking with his sword, and nearly drowning in the hot blood of his foes.

Barkov led a cohort of shielded men with swords. They were following the phalanx led by Ky, but as the ocean tide receded, there emerged a gap along the right side of the causeway, and Barkov took advantage. He urged his men forward, and they moved quickly past the fighting. Once near the island, they came up by the luggage, and he and his men gave a fierce battle cry.

The enemy was taken by surprise and fumbled to form up a defense. Barkov drove into the heart of the camp, lopping off limbs with his weapon. His men were close behind.

Two men in colorful, yet dirty, robes rushed from a tent.

Swarms of flying objects came stinging men with their barbed tails of bright red light. From behind the camp, four-legged metal creatures with long necks and fangs rushed the warriors. The robed men were muttering in tongues and waving their hands about. Barkov knew that these evil wizards summoned and controlled the demons.

A flying stinger cut into his flesh at his wrist, but it could not penetrate the magic armor. He charged hard into the monsters with his shoulder and drove it to the ground with a loud clack. More came at him, but he ignored his own mortality and swung his murderous sword. He cleaved one in twain, and sparks and lightning erupted from its metallic body. Looking up, Barkov saw the robbed figures begin to move back. He knew the time was right to strike.

With all his strength, he leapt over two of the charging monsters and rushed at the wizards. The men turned and began running. Unfortunately for them, their speed of egress was no match for Barkov's fleet of foot. He overtook them in seconds, and with two swipes of his blade, he took one's head and another's leg.

The wizard pulled his hood down, agony written upon his face. As he clutched at his bloody leg stump, Barkov rendered the fatal blow, sending the unnatural being to his doom.

Spinning around, Barkov prepared to engage the metal monsters, but they were now silenced and stood dumb to the world. He approached and slayed each as he went until there remained none standing.

HELON STRUCK HARD, driving Trecot back against some rocks. His eyes were fixed for murder and his mouth spouted curses. He summoned a beast from the sea, and its metal legs and mighty claws began to climb upon the land.

Warriors screamed as the creature came forth. Tall as a siege tower, it made its way up onto the rocky ground. Helon moved away fast and shouted, "Kill! Kill Trecot now!"

Trecot looked surprised. He knew that most priests had an ace in the hole. They kept ancient tools around them close at hand in case they were needed. This was clearly Helon's, and it was orientating to tear Trecot to shreds.

"Sorry to see you go, Trecot, but your time is at hand. The metals of your body will be missed, but it is a small matter!" Helon shouted as he rushed away.

The monstrosity stepped onto the land bridge, and the ground shook as it put the full weight of one foot down next to Trecot.

A beam of light erupted from the monster's eye. Men coming to Trecot's aid melted into ash. Trecot rushed between the giant's legs. The thing was confused for a moment, suddenly looking down and lifting one leg at a time, trying to stomp its target.

Sala watched helplessly as the creature attempted to crush his mentor. In a flash of insight, he closed his eyes and reached out into the ether with his mind. There, in the darkness, he found a light. From the light, he felt along its length to the source of the monster's intellect. Tapping into the gargantuan, he spoke into it, instructing the giant to murder its master.

The metal giant stopped and looked about. Its gaze fell upon Helon.

"No! Strato, you are to destroy Trecot, not I!"

A sharp sound blasted from the giant as it turned its hulking body and began stomping toward its former master. Helon fled toward the island. The priest shouted curses as he dodged massing men, thrust spears, and swinging swords. His flailing robe moved like a banner in the wind as he made it to the base of the far hill and started to climb.

The beast, without regard for those in its path, strode across the bridge after the fleeing wizard. Many of the enemy were crushed under its clawed metal feet. Once across the causeway, it pursued the fleeing priest with great dispatch.

Ky shouted, "Rally to me!" Rush the enemy!"

The city warriors drove the enemy toward the island. Somewhere near the rolling island hills, they drove the enemy upon the swords of Barkov and his men.

"It is a rout! The foes now defile themselves and rush to the hinterlands!" Barkov shouted. "I cut down at least a hundred. Maybe more."

Ky nodded. "I, too, have a high count of the dead. Those still alive lay in our wake even now, surrendering to our cohorts. Let them pray for mercy to the heathen god the copper men keep."

Trecot came up. He walked through the throng and stopped before the two warriors. "Be stoic! Now comes the king and his men. They, too, have bloodied their blades against the forces of the Golans. It is time to let the dying die and give mercy to those who will still live. Do not let the reckless lust of death lead you from your humanity."

Barkov frowned. What does Sala say? Does he keep such ideals as you? If we let them live, they might come again, and with greater numbers."

"The king will have the final say. Those left on the battlefield, our valiant foes, may be enslaved or forgiven. For the Golans make warriors by conscript, and those who refuse are put to the sword. So, do not be hasty, brave Barkov, to cut the throats of your enemies."

Harrumphing, Barkov sheathed his sword and folded his arms over his ample chest. "What nonsense," he said to Trecot.

The king approached. His men were armored and armed with lance and blade. Crimson droplets and gore were present on all.

"You two foreigners who led some of our men. I Prais you for your valor. Once the enemy are sorted you are invited to the feast I shall throw because of our victory. There, I shall pay you a bounty of brass so heavy that you may have trouble carrying it from the city."

Ky stepped forward. "It is our stock and trade, great king. Commanding men in battle comes as naturally to us as drinking wine and pawing women."

The king chuckled. "So, you say. What is your name, young warrior?"

"I am called Ky."

"And I am called Barkov the Beast." Barkov kept his arms folded.

"Our rear guard rounds up stragglers. The fleet of ships are either sank, on fire, or fled to the horizon. When the fire disk dreams this night, it will mark our victory. Come to the Great Hall and join with my nobles and warriors. There will be pickled lok, and meats of all types. Drink will be so plentiful you could bathe in it. Women and men will be brought in from the brothels, and star root will fill many a reed." He turned to Trecot. "You, old friend. Bring your acolyte. He is welcome too for his part."

"I do not have an acolyte, great king," Trecot stated.

The king looked confused. "He is not your protégé?"

"He, oh dread lord, is not an acolyte...at least not anymore. He is now a priest. He has now spoken to our god and wears the trappings of a learned one."

The king laughed. "Bring him! There will be enough to spare for all." He turned and led his warriors from the field back to the city.

"Well, you did me good service, brutes," Trecot said. "Your efforts will live on in song, I think. Anyway, it is time to enjoy the king's good mood. Follow. Remember to give mercy to those we pass still on the field."

Trecot led the way as the king's soldiers were busy with the work of retrieving fallen weapons and removing bodies. Once in the city, Barkov, Ky, Sala, and Trecot made use of the common bath complex.

Once done, Trecot separated from his companions, leaving Ky, Barkov, and Sala to get dressed for the festivities. They arrived at the feast just after the rise of the two moon gods in the evening sky.

Chapter 10

The Wake Left Behind

"EVERY ACTION LEAVES a record. The Golans kill and leave in their wake ruin that cries revenge. A cruel man beats his wife and, in his wake, grows the child who will do ill. The copper men come and transform children into monsters, and one day, there will rise from that wake a priest who will undo the copper men. Steady your life. Keep on an even keel. Ford troubled waters, and weather harsh storms. When you look ahead, remember that behind you is a wake that will follow you until you rot."

~ Proverb found in the pages of the book *Hu Tu Chronicles*, author unknown.

KY AND BARKOV STOWED their divine gifts in a locked chest at the temple, then walked back to the inn, where they sought their young friend.

Sala waved the two warriors over. "What do you hear upon the wind?" he asked as a waft of gray smoke passed over him from the fire pit.

"Scouts have reported that the Golan forces are attacking other walled cities. The king here will send some soldiers to help repel the attacks," Ky said.

"What of the sailing ships? Who sails to the western islands?" Sala asked.

"A trading ship sails for the west from the city's harbor this day. It is called *The Limpet*."

Sala chuckled. "From the first moment we met, our lives were intertwined. Our goals aligned. I know you desire brass for service, but there is much more left to do. Come with me, and there will be more fighting, more brass, and more glory for you. I swear it."

"Our apologies, young priest." Barkov sarcastically said while added a low bow. "But you were a sapling when we found you, and you are barely more at the rise of the day's fire disk. Why should we follow you?"

Sala thought about this. "It is true you rescued me. But, since then, I have led you to this place. Since, my knowledge has grown – and if I led you well before, just think on how well I will lead in the future." He smiled and handed Ky and Barkov each a reed of star root.

Barkov lit the end of the reed and drew in the pungent smoke. "I guess we have much to still teach you of surviving in the wilds, and we will accept your wisdom as it relates to our needs." He looked at Ky who nodded back. "Then it is settled. You'll lead, and we'll teach. And, there better be much brass we will gain when all is done."

Sala smiled and nodded. "Well put, my saviors. Now, let us gather your treasure and belongings and make for the docks. That land in the west calls me, and I must answer. It is there, beyond the edge of the world, we must go. There is still time to destroy the mother of the copper men and cripple the battle lust of the Golans, and men like Helon."

Trecot approached. He yawned, covering his mouth with his hand. "The old ones speak in your ear, and you are off to answer the call? I am sure you do well among the copper men. I travel also this day. The Golans come to strangle another city far to the south. There I go—and without your beasts to help me." He pointed to Barkov and Ky.

"What of Helon?" Sala asked.

"He will be licking his wounds for some time. I will not see him until Herod and Marjup again watch us with their full faces. He will be ready to meet me then, and I will be ready to mete out his doom. Fair winds and blessings be upon you. I will check in on your progress. Answer when I speak your name." Trecot turned, headed off toward a hallway, and vanished into the darkness of the passage.

THOSE WHO CELEBRATED the victory over the Golans littered the street as if they had fallen randomly from the sky. Sala and his companions wove their way through the aftermath toward the many ships moored at the city docks that jutted into the rocky cove.

In the distance, the sounds of the shifting wooden boats echoed, and in the air, the smell of rotting seagrass and fish was ripe. None stirred as they passed.

Once on the boardwalk, they found several sailors awake and tending to shipboard business.

"You!" called Barkov, who shouldered their locked box of brass ingots. "I see your ship sits low in the water. When will this galley take to the sea?"

"It is made this day for travel. We make for the Heart Islands to trade Hap Fro wood for spices. Do you seek passage there?" the old sailor replied.

"We do wish to book passage. Do ships sail beyond the Heart Islands?" Sala asked.

"Not if they be sane. Mostly pirates and slavers pass the Heart," said the sailor.

"Good," Sala stated. "Take us to the Heart, and we will see what foul fiends will carry us further on."

The sailor cracked a smile and shook his head. "Come aboard. We sail with the tide. Carpor, make a space on the deck for our passengers." He turned to Sala. "You will find a nice place to sleep on the side of the deck by the prow."

The ship pushed off the docks, the wind was blowing gently. They put out the oars and slowly made headway over rippling waters out to the crashing waves of the dark blue ocean.

When they made contact with the rolling surf outside the harbor, the ship nosed up, then down, and continued like that until it broke out into deep waters. The wind shifted.

Carpor and his mates put up the sails, stowed the oars into their hooks, and the ship lurched onward. Sala looked aft as the city and the land grew smaller. The fire disk was approaching straight up, and the cool wind scoured the decks.

"The mother of the copper men must be dealt with if I am to fulfill my purpose," Sala said into the wind.

"Mother? Copper men have mothers?" Ky asked.

"Only one mother. She lives underground. Upon the far shores of a land called Ostomark, her children reign supreme. Men and women who live there tend to her needs."

"What of our talents?" Barkov asked.

"Be calm. Be wary. If we do not draw attention to ourselves, we will meet the mother, and she will not be able to sound the alarm until it is too late," Sala replied.

Ky sat down. "And why is this important?"

"It marks the end of the old world. The monsters that steal children will be no more, and their power to make wizards—or, rather, priests—will be at an end. The Golans will find one less ally. That will shake up the Golan alliance and sow chaos in their ranks. It gives us—those who fight against the Golans—an edge."

Barkov nodded. "It is a good strategy. Then what of us? And what of Trecot? Do we meet and fight the Golans again? Or do we commit some skullduggery and hide in the shadows?"

"Let the gods decide that. I am only their servant. I will pray. If they take pity upon me, they will tell me what comes after," Sala stated.

THE SHIP SAILED FOR nine days. Two small storms filled the sky with lightning and hard rain that fell in sheets. In the distance, the boatswain sighted other ships, and weapons were passed out in case of pirate attack.

Upon the tenth day, land was spotted, and the flag that marked the lands of Heart soared above the battlements of the city. By nightfall, they arrived and disembarked. All manner of foreign people lurked about. Skins, hair, and eyes of many colors roamed the narrow streets of the small city.

Much trade came with the many ships anchored in the protected cove. Sala made for a structure built upon stilts on a hill. A shingle hung outside with the image of a bloody heart on it. Rough-looking men and women came and went.

"This is it," Sala proclaimed.

"It?" Ky asked.

"This is indeed it," Sala repeated.

"Enough riddles, priest!" Barkov said annoyed. "Spit it out plain!"

"Some find solace in the temples. They pray to their gods and seek forgiveness or absolution. Some do so in the wilds of the many lands that make up our world." He pointed at Ky and Barkov. "And there are some who seek resolute mercy in the arms of fermented grain or the juice of the berry. We seek such a man, and he will take us to the city of Vep among the coastal hills of Ostomark."

"A sailor?" Ky asked.

"No. A lost soul. A fallen priest who took refuge upon the seas to avoid being murdered. His salvation comes, and I am the one bringing it to him. He will, in turn, show us to an ancient cave. Inside, deep below, I will secure the means to kill the mother of the copper men."

"I shall take her head!" Barkov declared.

Sala found a seat and sat. "She has no head. She has no arms, legs, hands, or feet. Yet, she bore a race of monsters that still drive men to murder, women to despair, and children into hiding."

Barkov sat, as did Ky. A young boy came and set a pitcher of beer on the table along with three mugs.

"Who is this priest you speak of?" Barkov asked.

He was the first one to find the records. His name is Kador son of Landor, and he is the one who woke Trecot, and by extension me, exposing us to the wider truths and evils of the copper men." Sala picked up his beer and drank its contents. He raised his arm and called to a passing servant. "Bring more drink to this table, for our time here will be long, and our mouths dry from much talk."

The young woman nodded and headed off into the crowd, only to return hence with several jars of beer and berry wine.

"What more, priest?" Barkov asked while tipping a cup of wine to his lips.

Sala looked at the servant girl. "Bring meat, star root, and paramours. Upon their arrival, we will compensate your master well."

She looked on with an expression of mirth. "You may show me your brass now, for my master would say that promises are many, but brass pays the way." She looked down at Sala. "Do you know the master of this tavern?"

"Kador? I do! Bring him forth and we will drink and speak with him. Tell him that Sala the priest comes and he brings word of the downfall of the copper men" Sala said.

Don't miss out!

Visit the website below and you can sign up to receive emails whenever Lawrence BoarerPitchford publishes a new book. There's no charge and no obligation.

https://books2read.com/r/B-A-MRTR-JZUYC

BOOKS 2 READ

Connecting independent readers to independent writers.

Did you love *Sala The Acolyte*? Then you should read *The Leftover World*[1] by Lawrence BoarerPitchford!

In the past, a once thriving world fell into darkness. Hundreds of years later those survivors cobbled together civil townships upon the backs of child slaves. Dallas was placed into the care of the ranch – a place for orphans to be rented as chattel, to be used by farms and mines, often at the expense of kindness and patience.

---

1. https://books2read.com/u/mv9Eee

2. https://books2read.com/u/mv9Eee

In this world there is little hope for a life of willful determination and self-imposed destiny. But, there are some who by strength of will break their bonds and flee from the ranch. They are pursued by their guards and fall headlong into a coming war.

Standing between the primitive farming communities and destruction are a handful of youngsters led by a rogue army officer. He called himself a ranger, and taught his recruits the woodland arts, but will they be able to stem the tide of a conquering army bent on making one man the dictator over what remains of all the fallen colonies?

Will those who ran off the ranch, a band of rangers, reborn into this violent land, wield the tech of old, and retake the lands lost to them, and time?

Read more at https://www.boarerpitchford.com.